The Sword in the Roses

A Stolen Royalty Novella

By Autumn Kaufer

ISBN: 979-8-8691-8785-7
Cover image & design by: A.R. Kaufer
Courting Books Publishing
First edition, March 15th, 2024

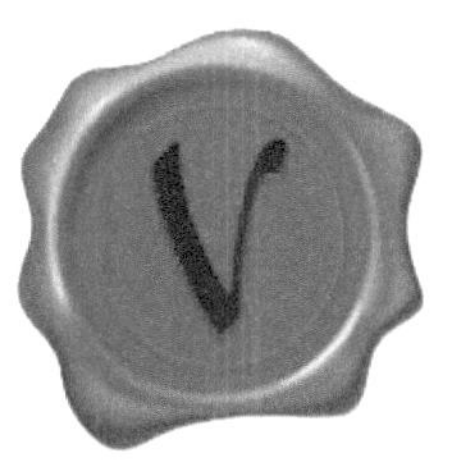

From the Library

of

Prince Dracke

This history has been translated by an author of the mortal realm to the best of her ability....

Prologue

Once upon a time

There is one universal truth known among the fae courts: fae cannot lie. This has led to battles, murder out of jealousy or hate, and assassinations.

All four courts, Fire, Wind, Earth, and Water, are in a constant struggle for power. A union between two of them might help bring the peace after a thousand years at war.

Princess Wisteria, daughter of Tristan, king of the Fire Court, had been informed only two weeks prior she would be married off to Grand Earl Mal of the Wind Court.

"Wisteria, please, be reasonable."

"Mother, how else should I be? I met him last week, and it was positively awful! I cannot marry him."

Wisteria studied her mother for a moment. Both had the same bright red hair, pale skin, and stunning blue eyes. Her mother's posture and countenance was that of nobility, never betraying her emotions. Unless it came to her rebellious daughter.

Delilah sighed. "Your father will not hear any more talk of your refusal. The betrothal will be formally announced in the morning. It is out of both our hands, I'm afraid."

"Mal is cruel beyond words. I cannot be bound to a male such as him. Please, help me make Father see reason," Wisteria pled with wide eyes.

Delilah's expression softened, and for a brief moment, Wisteria had a sense of hope. Until she shook her head. "I'm sorry, my dear. There is nothing to be done. You will marry him, and that is final." Before Wisteria could protest, her mother abruptly left the room.

The thought of marrying Mal nearly caused Wisteria to lose her stomach contents. She rushed to the bed, fell to her knees, and pulled out what she'd been working on before her mother came in. Jessiah, her friend and loyal handmaid, handed her a small bundle of clothing. Wisteria packed it into her bag.

"Thank you," she said with a smile.

"Be safe, mi'lady," Jessiah offered with a bow.

Wisteria glanced around one last time. Though this had been her home for over two hundred years, it never felt like such. Her chambers were grandiose, with white marble walls and matching floor, black and orange covers on the poster bed, and the washroom with the large, clawfoot tub.

With a dull ache in her chest, she tossed the sheets she'd tied together out of the window, threw the knapsack on her back, and quickly shimmied down to the ground.

She rushed towards the faery gate which would take her to the mortal realm. Her kind weren't exactly welcome there, but they weren't shunned, either. Anything would be better than the forced betrothal her parents chose for her.

The sun continued its slow descent as she moved swiftly through the woods. The soft leather pants and cotton tunic she wore afforded her fluidity in her movement. Her mind battled her heart at the thought of leaving, and she knew her family would be angry when they discovered her disappearance. Though she made her protestations known to them, they did not care.

Wisteria longed to marry for love. Her own parents' marriage had been arranged, but over time, they loved each other dearly. It's what she deserved as well. She would not settle for anything less.

She would hide in the mortal realm until she could figure out a plan. The thought brought her a small measure of comfort. At best estimate, she figured a few weeks, possibly a month would give her the time she needed. Surely no longer.

Chapter 1

A Year Later

$\mathfrak{R}$hea worked ten hours each day in the bakery. She swore she would smell like pastries for the rest of her life. The thought made her laugh to herself, but she couldn't complain. Things had gone well for her so far. She'd arrived at the village roughly a week after entering the realm.

Though known for its sweeter treats, the owner had been most impressed with her braided breads. They usually sold out each morning within an hour of opening. Rhea maintained the same routine, making the dough, helping at the register, then icing the remaining pastries after the morning rush.

She loved interacting with the regular customers who came in. There was the old widower who flirted with her, the young mother with twin boys who enjoyed the sugar rush, and of course, the teacher who drank more coffee in one sitting than Rhea would all week.

Between the long days and the magic she had to use, her body began to wear down. The spell helped hide her fae features and ward her so she could not be detected by the royal guards who must surely be searching for her.

She had been looking forward to her day off. That morning, however, the baker sent a messenger asking if she could come in. She smiled at him as he awaited her response. After thinking about it for a moment, she made her decision.

"Yes, tell him I'll be there shortly."

"Thank you."

She finished her breakfast and dressed before making her way. The bakery being nearby, she made the trip in less than five minutes.

"Oh, am I glad to see you! Livia fell ill, and I was afraid I would be by myself."

"Where is Olden?" Rhea asked, taking in the disheveled appearance of Sylvan. His apron was covered in flour, and his short dark hair went in a hundred different directions. Apparently, he'd been there all night baking.

"At the summer solstice festival in Lyouns."

"Oh, right!"

"I am so sorry to ask you to come in on your one day off this week."

Rhea gave him a sympathetic smile then tied on her apron. The cozy bakery had plenty of natural light from the two large windows on either side of the entrance. Its oak counter, walls, and floors were highlighted by the sunshine streaming in.

She went right to it, kneading the dough while Sylvan stoked the fires in the open-air ovens. They worked through the morning, pausing to greet customers and eat. At four o'clock, he locked the door.

"We'll close a bit early. I don't think anyone will mind, as most people have gone to the festival anyhow. You can go ahead. Thank you for your help."

"Are you sure? There's still the cleanup—"

"I insist. You appear a little under the weather, yourself. Take tomorrow off, and get some rest. I'll see you on Thursday."

"Thank you."

"No, please. You saved me today."

She untied her apron and left the bakery through the back door. Exhaustion rolled over her, and she leaned against the wall for a moment. The spell continued to take its toll on her.

If she could make it home, she would sleep. The rest would help recharge her, both her body and magic. She pushed away and started her walk through the quiet village.

She turned onto the road that led to her cottage. Warily, she glanced around before continuing on her way. The hairs on the nape of her neck stood on end. Perhaps someone was watching.

With a quiet laugh, she shook her head, reassuring herself it wasn't the case. Still, she glanced back from time to time, checking in between the thick trees that lined both sides of the path. Her walking slowed, her feet dragging as though moving through quicksand. After stumbling twice, she caught herself and managed to keep upright.

The cottage appeared on the horizon. Her pace quickened, and she knew she had to make it inside. It had its own ward, to help hide her while she slept. If she passed out before reaching it, she knew someone would find her.

Her home was small, round, and made of large river rocks mortared together. The wooden roof had been sealed to keep out the rain. For the finishing touch, the walls were insulated to help maintain its interior temperature. It was the only structure on the lane, affording her the privacy she needed. She hoped it also made it harder for anyone coming to the village to search for her.

When her legs finally gave out, she tumbled towards the ground. She braced herself, but right before she would hit, strong arms gathered her up. Fear seared through every nerve.

"Who are you?" she demanded, twisting to look at whoever held her. His firm grip made the movement impossible. "What do you want?"

"Is this your cottage?" the male asked. She stiffened in response. "I'll take that as a yes. Let's get you inside."

Cradled in his arms, he kept her face buried against his chest. He opened the door and took her to the chair by the fireplace. After settling her in it, he started a fire. Rhea kept her fear at bay and prepared herself to question him.

"Do I know you?" she asked.

"No. I was out hunting," he said as he slipped off his bow and quiver to lay by the door. "I saw you, and I could tell you weren't going to make it on your own. Had a little too much to drink at the tavern?" He chuckled.

"I'm not drunk," she said with a yawn, clearly struggling to stay awake.

"Are you sure?" The flames roared to life as he stood to face her. "You don't look very well."

"I'm drained and need sleep. Please, leave now."

"When's the last time you ate?" he asked, making his way to the small, open kitchen. Vegetables were laid out, along with a few other ingredients.

"I ate a sandwich at eleven."

"You need to eat. Were you going to make stew?"

"Yes, but—"

"I'll prepare it."

"Who are you?" she asked again.

"Apologies, I'm Argus."

"I'm Rhea."

"Pretty name."

He began to dice the tomatoes, glancing at her from time to time. Her sky-blue eyes caught his own amber ones. Her lips were the perfect shade of pink, and he couldn't help but stare. He pushed away his thoughts about them.

"Where did you learn how to cook?" she asked, yawning again.

"I'm trained in a variety of things. Now, shut your trap and get some rest. I'll wake you when dinner is ready."

"Hmm, so bossy," she mumbled, giving in to her exhaustion.

While she slept, he checked on the stew from time to time, then disappeared into her bedroom. He glanced over his shoulder while he packed her bag. Once he was certain she had what she would need, he placed it beside his own knapsack by the front door.

He brought in a bowl and set on the table next to her. After fixing himself some, he carried in a chair from the dining area. Careful not to wake her yet, he sat in front of her.

Studying her face, a small pang of guilt hit his chest. He didn't have a choice. This was nothing more than a job, and he would do whatever he must. He pushed it down, clearing his throat, and waking her.

"Dinner is ready." He nodded towards the bowl beside her.

She sat up and glanced at it before turning to him. "Thank you."

"You're welcome," he said as he wiped his mouth.

Not as tired now, Rhea took note of his appearance. His clothing consisted of simple brown leather pants, a cream-colored tunic, and a dark green cloak, which he'd hung on the hook by the front door.

"How did you find me?"

"I saw you," he said with a grin, as though he'd offered an inside joke.

"What do you do for a living, Argus?"

He blew on his spoonful of stew and looked pensive while trying to find the right words. "I am trained in many things. Right now, I'm hunting."

"Hence the bow." She took note of the full quiver on the floor. "You must not have had any luck today."

"What makes you say that?"

"It's still packed with arrows."

"You got me," he said with a smile, though it didn't quite reach his eyes. The peppermint tea rolled down his throat as he took another sip. "You said you worked in a bakery. How long have you worked there?"

"About a year." She moved as though to stand. He jumped up and took her dishes from her. "Thank you," she said with a yawn. "Sorry. I am still exhausted."

"Get some rest."

"Will I see you tomorrow?" she asked, hoping he would take the hint to leave for the night.

"I promise." He lifted the blanket to her shoulder and patted it gently. "You need to sleep now."

The room started to dim. She stared at him for a moment, wondering if he put something in her tea, but passed out before she could ask.

Argus stoked the fire before grabbing a book from the shelf to read while she slept. He glanced at her from time to time, trying not to stare, and failing. Her hair framed her face beautifully, and he wanted nothing more than to run his fingers through the red strands.

He shook his head and forced himself to pay attention to the story. Two hours later, he began to nod off as well. He knew Rhea would sleep through the night.

Rhea awoke with a start. She glanced around the cottage before noticing Argus in the chair. His intense expression caused her heart to pound furiously in her ribcage.

"You're still here?" she asked, trying to hide her confusion.

"I am."

She stretched and stopped when she saw the sunlight coming in. "It's morning!"

"You were exhausted."

"Or you put something in my food or tea," she said with an accusatory tone.

"We have a long day ahead of us and needed the rest."

"Well, thank you for staying. Will I see you around?" When he showed no inclination to leave, she tried to think of a polite way to ask him to go. "How can I ever repay you? Oh, perhaps tomorrow you could stop by the bakery, and I will buy you a pastry?"

"Why this village? And why a bakery of all places?"

A nervous laugh escaped her. "Whatever do you mean?"

"Why are you here?"

"I like the people. Sylvan, the owner, is truly kind. He took me right in and helped me get settled, him and his wife."

"Why did you leave the Fire Court?"

"The Fire Court?" she asked, a slight pitch in her voice. "What do you know about it?"

"Fae can't lie, so you use your workarounds. It's annoying, by the way."

"How do you know?"

He ran his hand through his mahogany brown hair, which stopped inches above his shoulders, and revealed his own pointed ear. "Now, Princess. Are you ready to go back?"

Her jaw dropped, but before she could respond, he bound her in iron wrist cuffs. "Who are you?" she demanded while struggling to break free of his grasp.

Argus lifted her from the chair then slammed her into it when she kicked and squirmed. "We can do this the easy way or the hard way. That's up to you." His eyes narrowed. "But you are coming with me."

When he lifted his pack, she noticed her own bag beside it. Once he secured them, he reached for her.

"Don't touch me!" she screamed.

"Very well. The hard way it is."

"No!"

He lifted her over his shoulder and carried her from the cottage. Rhea continued to cry out and squirm. This was the one time she wished she weren't so isolated from the village. No one would hear her, so no one would come to her rescue. Argus let out a loud whistle. A moment later, a large, white steed approached them.

"Good boy." Argus sat Rhea on the saddle before securing their packs on either side. "Now, Princess, if you behave, you won't get leg shackles or a gag. Hmm, the thought of seeing you in such a predicament does things to me," he said as he joined her.

Her back stiffened against his chest. "I'll do whatever you ask, but please. Do not take me back."

"Beg all you like. It will make no difference. This task is mine, and I will complete it. You are a thing to be bartered with, nothing more. I suggest you quiet down and enjoy the trip. It's a long way to the faery gate."

"I don't understand. Why don't you vaolmerse us there?"

He chuckled softly. "Those shackles you're in? They are pure iron and will suppress your magic. Not just yours though, but anyone in close proximity. It is impossible to teleport ourselves, so we have to do it the old-fashioned way. Should only take about a week, then you'll be free of me."

"If you complete this task, I will never truly be free."

"Ask me if I care."

Her shoulders sagged, and she gasped when his arm wrapped around her waist to move her back flush against his torso. The well-worn path led them to the village. Once they approached, the horse turned left.

"I can't leave without saying goodbye."

"Too bad."

The tears she fought to keep at bay sprung free, falling down her cheeks. "Please, I would rather die than return to the Fire Court."

"I don't think such dramatics are necessary, Princess. Believe me, there is nothing you can say or do to change my mind."

"I… I can pay you!"

His chest vibrated with laughter at her suggestion. "Oh, I think not."

"But I mean it. I—"

"No, you misunderstand. What they are paying me, there is nothing comparable you could offer. Shut your mouth."

Her tears landed on his arm, and he wiped them away before glancing at the thick woods surrounding them.

"Where are we?" she asked, realizing she'd lost sense of direction.

"We are west of your little village, heading for Lyouns. There, we will rest for tonight then continue tomorrow. From Lyouns to the next village, Seigne, there is a three-day trail through woods, plains, and rivers. Tonight will be our last night sleeping indoors for a while."

"You can't do this. I command you to let me go."

"My orders come from someone with higher authority than you." He reached into his pocket to show her the gag. "Keep it up, and I won't hesitate to use this on you."

Her eyes went wide as her head lowered.

Chapter 2

The Festival

They arrived at Lyouns, with the summer solstice festival in full swing. They heard the music and applause as they rode towards the business end of the village. Argus removed a jacket from his knapsack and covered Rhea's bindings. After helping her dismount, he laced his arm with hers.

Together, they went to the only inn they saw. It was a large, dark brown structure. To Rhea, it loomed over her, threatening her. She shook her head, telling herself she would not give in to her fear. Controlling her emotions was what she should focus on.

They approached the counter, where an older gentleman waited for them. After explaining they needed a room for the night, he removed a key from the small wooden box on the counter.

"I only have one left. Busy time, as you see."

"It's fine," Argus said as he took it. He scanned the dinner menu on the counter, pointed to what they wanted, and smiled at the innkeeper.

"Someone will bring that in shortly."

"Good man."

Argus led Rhea to their room. He unlocked the door and shoved her inside.

"You have to be kidding me!" she exclaimed when she realized there was only one bed.

Argus glanced around, taking note of the windows and scanning for any other exits. "What's the matter?"

"I am not sleeping with you," she declared. Her chin jutted towards the bed.

"No one said you are. You will sleep on the floor while I enjoy the cozy bed."

"Tell me you're joking."

"Hmm, did you want to snuggle with me, Princess?"

Rhea gagged. "Shut up!" Noticing the washroom, she let out a sigh. "We haven't stopped since lunch! I need to… you know." She nodded towards the door.

"Then go."

She held up her arms. "Undo these."

"I can't, I'm afraid."

"But—"

"Will you go already?" he snapped.

Without another word, she went inside. She managed to relieve herself and wash her hands, though it wasn't without difficulties. The water flowed from the tap, hot and clear. She gathered it up to clean her face.

A knock at the door caused her to jump. "Hey, you aren't the only one who needs to use this. Hurry up before I join you."

His threat met its target, and she returned to the main chamber. He took her to the bed, forced her to sit, and removed a chain from his knapsack. Using a small padlock, he attached it to her irons after running it through the metal headboard.

"Stay," he commanded.

"Like I have a choice," she said as she rattled them at him.

As soon as the door shut, she pulled with every ounce of strength she could muster. They would not budge. There had to be a way to free herself. She focused on her magic, but nothing happened.

The disconnect left her empty, and a feeling of despair unlike any she'd known before threatened to swallow her whole. After using her magic regularly for the past year, the sudden loss punched a hole in her heart. She swore she would do whatever she must in order to regain her power.

The door opened, and her eyes remained on the floor as he stepped up to her. "Dinner will be here shortly. We can freshen up after, then we'll turn in."

"I am not sleeping like this," she hissed at him.

"Of course not, Princess."

"Stop calling me princess!"

"Why? It's your title, isn't it?"

"I left that life behind."

"I can't wrap my head around that. Why would you rather work in a hot bakery all day than live a life of luxury?"

"Royal life isn't all it's cracked up to be, I assure you."

"Oh, yes. To have large chambers with a soft bed, to never know what it is to be cold or hungry. It sounds positively dreadful."

Her steeled gaze met his, with disdain clear on her face. "You don't know anything about me!" Her breath heaved as her lips trembled. "You know nothing of what my life was like there. At least working in the bakery is *my* choice."

"Foolish little girl. You threw away what so many can only dream of having."

She shook her head. "Nothing I say will convince you, so why waste my breath?" A knock at the door startled her.

"Food is here." Argus opened it, took the tray, and thanked the woman.

He carried it to the small table in the corner before returning to Rhea. After unlocking the padlock, he left it hanging with the chain. They sat down to eat.

"Why do I have to eat stew while you get steak?"

The knife in his hand glinted as he angled it in the light. "Why do you think?"

"It's not fair. I want steak."

"Gods, you really are a demanding brat. Fine." He cut a piece and offered it to her on his fork. For a moment, she debated it, thinking he must surely be tricking her. When he didn't move, she accepted it. "Better?" he asked as he continued to cut his meat.

"It's delicious. I haven't had any in a long time."

"Who's fault is that?"

Her gaze went to her tea, and she said nothing else as she took a sip. The silence between them stretched on while they ate. When she finished, she glanced down at her dirty garments.

"I need to wash up and change into fresh clothes."

"There is a communal bath here. We will clean up before we turn in."

Her meal threatened to rise up her throat. "We?" she squeaked out.

"Yes, but not to worry. We will each use a stall or take a turn, depending on the setup."

"Thank you." A bang in the hallway drew their attention. When he turned to look, she snatched away his knife, and held it on her lap. "Probably a drunk from the festival," she said with a laugh.

He chuckled before resuming his meal. He lifted his plate then his napkin. His eyes met hers, and it was obvious he realized what she'd done. Before she could utter a word, he lunged across the table, knocking everything off with a clatter. He pressed her against the wall.

In the blink of an eye, she aimed the blade of his steak knife at his throat. The serrated edge brushed against his stubble.

"Release me," she demanded.

"No."

"I will not hesitate." The sharp metal pressed deeper, drawing a thin trail of blood.

"Looks to me like you already did." His arm wrapped around her waist, drawing her closer to him. "As you can feel, I am enjoying this immensely."

Her face twisted with disgust. Using the temporary distraction, he spun her around, so her back pressed against the wall with the tip now at her neck.

"Little advice, Princess. When you have the chance to kill someone, you take it. Don't delay, even for a moment. It's how you get yourself killed."

"You sound as though you are speaking from experience," she said, glancing at the hand gripping the knife.

"Oh, don't worry. I have to bring you back alive and unharmed." He tossed it onto the table. "We need to clean up after the mess you made."

"Me?"

"It wouldn't have happened if you didn't try to kill me, would it?"

"No, I guess not."

He grabbed a handful of clothes from each bag and piled them into her arms, effectively hiding her bindings. They stepped out into the hallway.

They were near the bath when a maid walked towards them. Argus turned on his charming smile. "I'm sorry to bother you. We are in room 5, and we got a little carried away. Didn't we?" He kissed the back of Rhea's head. "Would you mind to clean it up for us?" he asked as he squeezed Rhea's elbow.

She also smiled. "We would greatly appreciate it."

The maid nodded. "Of course."

"Thank you," Argus said.

When they arrived at the bath, relief flooded over Rhea to see they were the only ones. She set the pile of clothing on a shelf beside the stalls. He led her into one of them. After a moment, she sighed.

"Please?" she asked, holding up her arms. He began to undress her. "What… What are you doing?" When he didn't answer her, she took a step backward. "Don't do this."

He grabbed her wrist and jerked her forward before he continued. "I wasn't going to. Since you can't be trusted, you leave me no choice."

The gown fell away, and he made no effort to hide his satisfaction at seeing her in only her corset and undergarment.

"I'll let you keep those. At least, this time." He turned on the water and began to unbutton his shirt.

"What are you doing?" she asked softly.

"I told you, we need to get clean."

"No. I am not showering with you. Go to the next stall. I promise, I'll behave. You know I'm telling the truth."

"Princess, that ship has sailed."

He stripped down completely, and she kept her eyes averted, not wishing to see any part of him. After removing the sandalwood soap from the waxy paper, he lathered it between his palms.

While washing her body, he made sure to take care of where his hands moved. Part of her was repulsed, but a small, secret part she would be loath to confess, couldn't help but enjoy each caress. His touch sent a spark through her, waking every nerve, and heat pooled in her core.

After he rinsed her hair, he handed her the soap. She tilted her head. "What am I supposed to do with this?"

His mouth stretched into a mischievous smirk. "I washed you. Now it's my turn."

Her jaw dropped. "You are disgusting," she said with a sneer.

"It's only fair," he said, stepping closer. "Think of it like this. Misbehave, and you will be punished." His lips brushed over her lower earlobe. "Be a good girl, and you'll be rewarded."

"Please, don't make me do this," she pled as she met his gaze.

He snatched it from her hand before forcefully turning her away from him. "Fine. Just stand there, won't take me but a minute."

"What is the mark on your chest?" When he didn't answer, she dared to glance back. His face contorted in anger. "I'm sorry. I shouldn't have asked."

Rhea said nothing else while he washed himself. When finished, he dried her first. She quickly dressed and said nothing on the walk to their chamber.

The maid had indeed cleaned up their mess. Argus led Rhea towards the bed, but she stopped walking.

"What are you doing?" she asked, crossing her arms over her chest.

"We need a good night of sleep before traveling tomorrow."

He pushed her forward, forcing her to her knees. Removing the chain and padlock from the headboard, he then proceeded to attach them to her cuffs, after wrapping it around the leg of the bed.

"Sleep tight."

She sat on the floor, looking at him with wide eyes. "You can't be serious."

"Would you rather cuddle?"

"Gods, you are so foul."

He chuckled softly as he went into the washroom. Trick or not, this could be her chance to escape. It took tremendous force, but she lifted the corner of the bed enough to remove her chain.

As soon as she was free, she made a beeline for the door. It didn't budge and took her a moment to realize it was locked. She moved the bolt and reached for the knob when strong arms wrapped around her waist, pulling her back, then throwing her onto the floor.

She landed with a thud, her head slamming down. Stars flew in front of her as pain washed over her. She managed to stand. Argus lifted her up. She used the momentum, bringing her knee to his chin before he could react.

Argus kept his grip on her, walked to the bed, and tossed her onto it. "What are you doing?" she cried out.

"I told you if you misbehave, you will be punished."

He chained her to the headboard then went to his knapsack. Rhea's eyes went wide at the sight of the gag and chains he brought to her.

After freeing her from the headboard, he chained her in such a way so she could only lie in a curled-up position. Next, he proceeded to gag her before placing her on the floor.

With the final chain, he wrapped it around the leg of the bed to keep her in place. He ignored the tears streaming down her cheeks, the hatred burning in her gaze, and the small sting of guilt hitting him at the sight.

"Try that again, I will not hesitate to hurt you," he threatened as he dimmed the light. She flinched when he climbed over her and onto the bed. "Now go to sleep."

Argus bolted upright at the sound of Rhea crying. He switched on the light before kneeling beside her. While removing the gag, he scanned for any blood or injuries.

"Are you hurt?" he asked when he didn't see any.

She kept her head down. "No."

"Then what's wrong?" He ran his fingers through his hair.

"Bad dreams. I… I didn't mean to wake you. I'm sorry."

"What was it about?"

She held up her wrists. "Please, take these off. I need to comfort myself the only way I know how."

"What do you mean?"

"It's a soothing spell. It doesn't take much magic and only takes a moment. Please?"

His expression softened. "I'm sorry, but I cannot. As a way to ensure I return you to the kingdom, I do not have the key to the cuffs themselves. Only your father has it."

"I need comfort." She shivered against him.

"Tell me about it."

"Please, no."

"Tell me now," he demanded.

Resolve steeled in her as she lifted her eyes to his. "I want to go back to sleep. I don't want to talk about it."

Argus sighed. "It's getting late." He undid the chains around her ankles, lifted her up, and placed her on the bed. "Lie here with me. I swear I will not touch you without your consent."

"Fine."

He dimmed the light once more before joining her. The heat radiating from him brought her a small measure of comfort, and she drifted off to sleep.

Rhea woke up first, surprised to find herself snuggled against Argus, his arm draped over her stomach. She cleared her throat to wake him.

He stretched and scooted backwards. "Well, at least you slept the rest of the night."

"Yes, thank you."

"Any time, Princess," he said as he helped her from the bed. "We'll eat breakfast then hit the road. It'll be a long, dull ride to the next town."

Rhea slipped into the washroom. The face peering back from the mirror belonged to a stranger. Between the bags under her eyes and the fear drawn across her visage, she did not even recognize herself.

She splashed some cool water on her face, dried it off, then joined Argus at the table. He glanced at the clock, tapping his foot, and growing impatient.

"Is something the matter?" she asked.

"The sign at check-in said breakfast is delivered daily by eight o'clock." He gripped her elbow and stood her up before proceeding to unlock the chain. "We'll get dressed then see about breakfast."

Rhea quickly changed when he turned away from her. She slipped into a turquoise gown with long sleeves, knowing it would help to hide her wrist cuffs. Protecting Argus was the least of her concern, but if someone saw them and tried to fight him, she didn't know what might happen, that he may even blame her.

Argus stepped up beside her, dressed in dark leather pants, a cream-colored tunic, and his green cloak. "Since your gown covers your wrists, I'll leave the chain off for the time being." His brow furrowed. "But do not get any ideas."

"I'll behave."

They left their chamber and went to the entrance of the inn. An older lady with silver hair tied up in a bun smiled from behind the counter as they approached her.

"How is your stay?" she asked.

Argus turned on his charm. "Now, how did you know we are already guests?"

She smiled at Rhea. "My husband told me about the lovely lady with red hair."

He couldn't help but chuckle. "Of course. Um, yes. Everything is okay, but we never received breakfast."

"Oh, my apologies! Ilias should've told you when you checked in, breakfast service is on hold this week due to the festival. There are several wonderful foods being served."

"I see. Thank you. We will head there now."

"Are you staying for another night?"

"No. We will return shortly," Argus answered.

"Then I shall have my porter take your belongings to the stable," she offered.

"Thank you."

Argus settled the bill then led Rhea outside. Music played nearby. She smiled at him.

"No."

"I didn't say anything."

Argus scoffed. "I know what you are thinking. We are getting a meal then heading out. This is not a vacation."

"But can we—"

"No," he repeated, abruptly cutting her off with a sharp look as well. "Eat and leave."

She swallowed hard but said nothing else. Everything bustled with excitement. Children ran by, fighting over who had the better sweet. The music grew louder as Rhea and Argus made their way to the heart of the village. They arrived at the food vendors. He ordered two plates then took her to an empty table.

Argus devoured his before glancing at Rhea's. "Something wrong with your meal?"

"No."

"You've hardly touched it."

"Why do you care?"

He leaned in close, his breath grazing her ear. "Because I am supposed to bring you back in pristine condition. Do you understand, Princess?"

"Stop calling me that."

"Hurry up and eat." His voice was gruff, and he took a sip of water to clear the frog in his throat.

He could tell she was reluctant to do so but relieved she didn't fight back. When she finally finished, they threw away their trash and headed for the stable.

Argus was shoved from behind, and he and Rhea ended up in the dance circle. She pulled away from him and kicked up her heels to the music, joining with the others in the crowd.

She shot him a sly smile as she spun and twirled to the rhythm. His fists clenched as tightly as his jaw, but he could only watch. Causing a scene was the last thing he needed.

The dancers clasped hands and went two laps around the fountain in a circle before being joined by their partners. Rhea ended up right in front of Argus, and he found himself enveloped in her embrace.

"What are you doing?"

She laughed at his question, ignoring it as she continued with the crowd. Argus kept her close to him, and when it came time to switch partners, he stared daggers at the man standing next to them. He yanked Rhea out of the circle.

"That was fun!"

"And a waste of time. We are already running behind."

"Don't be such a sourpuss."

Before he could respond, a young girl of at least eight years approached Rhea, holding something behind her back.

"You're so pretty!" the little blonde squealed.

"Thank you."

"I made this." She held up a crown of roses and daisies. "I want you to have it."

"That's too much for me," Rhea protested.

"It's just right," the little girl said.

Rhea knelt before her, smiling as the girl placed the crown on her head. She hugged the child before thanking her.

"There you are! Your father and I were worried sick." A blonde woman approached. From her appearance, there could be no doubt she was the little girl's mother.

She took her hand, smiled at them, then followed her mother back into the crowd. Rhea turned to Argus, ready to make a princess joke. The scowl on his face stopped her.

"What's wrong?"

He gripped her arm and practically dragged her to the barn. After thanking the stable hand, Argus watched him leave. Without warning, he snatched the crown from Rhea's head.

"What are you doing?" she asked, reaching for it. He threw it to the ground. She knelt down to retrieve it, but he stomped on it with his boot. Tears streamed down her face as she stood. "Why did you do that?"

He lifted her on the horse then mounted behind her. After reattaching her chains and hiding them under the cloak, they left the stable and headed for the path.

Rhea wiped her tears. "Why did you destroy my beautiful crown?"

Argus said nothing, which only scared her. She thought about asking again, but his arm tightened around her waist. Her breath whooshed from her.

"You're hurting me."

He remained silent, but his grip loosened. They rode through lunch and finally stopped at dinner. Rhea nearly fell from the mount.

"I'm about to burst!"

Argus escorted her into a thicket, standing back while she did what she needed to do. She walked to the creek and rinsed her hands. He lit a small fire, then set up their meal. She sat with her back to him, not eating or saying anything. He let out a loud sigh.

"Why aren't you eating?"

"I don't have an appetite."

"Is this because of what happened in the stable?"

"No, though I am still upset because of what you did. You are returning me to the Fire Court, right?"

"I am."

"Then I see no point in eating."

"What?"

"I told you I would rather die than go back there. I know what is in store for me. It is not a life I wish to live."

"I swear, you and your dramatics."

When she faced him, the pain in her gaze nearly froze his heart. "You know I speak the truth."

"Yes, but you have a certain flair about it."

She stood and took a few steps, her heart racing as her mind spiraled into despair. "You have no idea what my life has been like."

"Nor do I care. Do you think I want to hear how hard it is, having servants to wait on you hand and foot, wearing clothing worth more than most of us would make in a month? Pardon me if I don't shed a tear for you."

Rhea lost it. She spun on her heel. "That's all you think about, isn't it? How luxurious my life must be? Yes, why wouldn't I want to be used as a pawn in the war? Why don't I love the idea of being married to a male who only wants to use and degrade me?" Everything she'd kept bottled up this past year spilled out, unable to be contained even a moment longer.

Argus jumped to his feet. "What are you talking about?"

Rhea laughed. "Why do you think you're returning me?"

He opened his mouth, but nothing came out. The conversation he had with his uncle replayed in his mind. "I was told you disappeared. The king searched everywhere for you, but no one could find you. After time passed, they were desperate and running out of options. They sent me. What am I missing?"

Rhea debated but realized there was nothing to lose. She sat down, and he joined her, watching as she picked at the bread on her plate.

"I'm being forced into an arranged marriage."

"And? It's pretty standard with royalty."

The bread slipped from her hand. "Never mind," she said with a scoff. "I knew you wouldn't understand."

She started to stand when he laced his fingers with hers. "I'm sorry. Please, tell me about it."

Her shoulders sagged as she pulled away. "Very funny. Why are you so cruel?"

He instantly moved beside her, his torso pressed against her back as he guided her to him. "I mean it."

"I'm betrothed to Mal."

"Wait, Grand Earl Mal of the Wind Court?"

"The very one. You know him?"

"I've heard the name."

"My parents informed me everything had been arranged. Then I had to meet him." She trembled against him. "It was the two of us. He… He forced me to…"

"Did he hurt you?"

"Not the way you're thinking. He forced me to undress so he could 'examine the goods' as he put it." Her breath shuddered. "Then he made me kneel. He bound me, similar to this." She held up her wrists. "I didn't understand what was happening. The next thing I knew, my neck was on fire, and I'm screaming in pain."

"What?" She lifted her hair. His fingers trailed over the mark at the nape of her neck. "The son of a bitch branded you?"

"Yes. He said once I am his wife, he will own me. That I will be at his disposal, to use, abuse, however he sees fit. My only purpose will be to lie on my back while he…" She buried her face in her hands.

"I'm sorry."

She wiped her tears as she faced him. "You're still taking me back, aren't you?"

"I have no choice."

"Gods, you are a despicable bastard. Do you not have even an ounce of compassion within you?"

"I never had the opportunity to learn it."

"What do you mean?"

He let out a sigh. "We need to get back on the road."

"I'm thirsty."

Argus removed his flask and handed it to her. Rhea greedily sipped the cool water. As she started to return it, she turned it over and pulled it closer to examine instead.

"This looks familiar."

Argus snatched it away. "I'm going to refill this. If you need to go, go. It'll be a while before we stop again."

They hurried their tasks then mounted the horse. Argus held her tightly against him, and Rhea didn't object this time. Something about his demeanor put her at ease as they rode toward the sunset.

After a few hours, Argus found a spot in the woods to set up camp. Rhea glanced around. "Where am I sleeping?"

"Where do you think, Princess?"

"Gee, what a gentleman."

"I didn't hear you complain last night."

She made an exaggerated gagging noise as she lay beside him. "Thank you."

"Whatever for?"

"I know it's your obligation, but I feel safe with you. Safer than I have in a long time. I've spent this past year looking over my shoulder, waiting for the day someone would find me. Though I hate it has happened, I'm glad it's you and not someone else."

"What do you mean?"

"Someone who would hurt me or use me. I know you are taking me back to barter, I heard you say that. Still, you haven't tried to take advantage of me. I know I shouldn't have to say thank you, but given how I've been treated in the past, I really do appreciate it."

"You're right. You shouldn't have to thank me. Still, I'm glad I'm the one who found you as well. Now shut up and go to sleep."

"So bossy," she said as she snuggled in closer with him, trying to warm herself from the nighttime chill in the air.

Chapter 3

The Truth

Rhea sat beside Argus as the fire died out. He finished his coffee. "Ready to hit the road?"

She laughed in response. "Like I have a choice."

"Good point." He tensed up when she scooted closer to him. "What are you doing?"

"It's frigid this morning, and I need to warm up."

He removed his cloak, wrapped it around her, then helped her stand. They walked to the horse, where he lifted her onto the saddle. Without much effort, he was instantly behind her.

"When will we see another village?"

"In about two days."

"Two days. I long for a soft bed and a hot bath."

Argus chuckled. "Not any time soon, I'm afraid."

They rode along the path, pausing for a quick lunch before resuming. After nearly an hour, Argus tugged on the reigns.

"Why did we stop?"

"Shh."

Rhea clamped her mouth shut as she glanced around. Nothing seemed out of place. "What's wrong?" she whispered.

"What do you hear?"

She listened for a few moments before shaking her head. "I don't hear anything."

"Exactly. No birds singing, no critters chittering."

"So something's wrong?"

"Yes, but I don't know—"

Before Argus could finish, an arrow penetrated Rhea's shoulder. She would've been knocked clean off if not for his arm around her waist. He dismounted, carefully helping her down. They took cover behind the nearest tree.

"Who are you?" Argus called out.

When no one responded, he examined her injury. She winced when his hand brushed the arrow. A bitter scent wafted to him, and his eyes went wide.

"They used poison. We have to get it out, stop the bleeding, then—"

Twang! An arrow splintered bark from the trunk of the tree they were hiding behind. Argus jumped to his feet and faced five bandits. They wore dark cloaks and were armed to the teeth. Swords, bows, and daggers were fully visible.

"What do you want?" Argus asked, staring at the one he assumed to be their leader.

The man stepped forward, proving Argus right. "We normally ask for a fee." He looked past Argus and smiled at Rhea. "But she will suffice. My men are lonely, after all."

"Over my dead body," Argus managed through gritted teeth.

"That can easily be arranged."

"Wait!" Rhea called out, slowly clambering to her feet. "How much is your fine?"

"Five hundred gold."

Argus gasped softly. "We do not have enough coin. Besides, given the poison used on the arrow that penetrated her, she doesn't have enough time to be of any use to you."

The leader laughed. "I have the antidote. Give her to us, and we will heal her. You will be free to go."

Rhea stepped back, her color gone, and her lips trembling. Argus gripped her wrist and pulled her forward. "I'm sorry."

"What?" she asked as he pushed her towards the bandits. "No!"

As soon as the leader reached for her, Argus shoved her behind him, planting his own dagger in the leader's throat. Argus managed to free the man's sword from its sheath as he crumpled to the ground.

Chaos erupted as steel and flesh met. Argus took out another bandit, swiping his blade across his stomach then kicking him to the ground. The third bandit approached, more cautious than the others.

Little good it did him when Argus rushed forward, catching him off guard, and cutting his leg. As he fell to the ground, Argus brought up his blade, running him through the ribcage.

He threw his body at the fourth bandit, who turned to avoid being caught under the dead weight. He lunged forward, and their swords clashed.

While they were distracted, the fifth bandit slowly circled around. He snatched Argus's dagger from the leader's throat. The other man kicked Argus backward, and he took advantage. He charged at Argus, dagger raised, when Rhea saw what was happening.

She jumped in front of Argus, causing the man to collide with her, and they fell to the ground together. The blade rammed into her stomach, and she cried out in pain.

Argus lifted his sword, decapitated his opponent, then rushed to Rhea and the last bandit, who lay beneath her. Argus carefully rolled her away, his breath sucking in at the sight. He ran his blade through the man's torso, pinning him to the ground.

Fear coursed through his veins as Argus went to the leader's body. He searched his pockets and small pouch, only to come up empty-handed.

"Where is the antidote?" he cried out as he searched the other bandits. Then it dawned on him. "It must be at their camp. I have no idea where they set up."

He snatched up the largest pouch after finding a few basic first-aid items. Rhea crumpled to the ground and whimpered in pain when the arrow snapped. Argus knelt beside her.

"You'll be all right," he assured her.

Time was running out, and the choice needed to be made. Should he stabilize the wound to her stomach first or continue his futile search for the antidote? She cried out softly when he moved her onto one of the bandit's cloaks.

Despair gripped his heart as her color faded fast. "Rhea, stay with me." He pulled out a small key, unlocked her bindings, and placed them in his pack, which he tossed several feet away.

"You… you said you didn't have the key to the wrist cuffs," she managed to get out.

"I lied."

"We… Impossible… Fae can't lie." Her body went limp in his arms.

He pulled away the remnants of the shaft from her shoulder. "Listen to me. The iron suppressed your magic, but now that it's gone, there should be a slight surge any moment. Use it to heal yourself."

"No."

"What?" he asked, swallowing hard in disbelief.

"I told you, I'll die before I will return to him."

"Rhea—"

"You can have my cottage. It's pretty in the spring when the roses are in full bloom."

"It sounds nice. Listen to me, focus. You have to heal yourself."

"No," she repeated with a shuddering breath.

"I can't do it, so you have to! Don't give up. Please, don't give up. I need you, Rhea."

Her eyelids fluttered then closed as blood continued to ooze from her wounds. Argus felt the small surge within himself, and he concentrated on it before speaking softly. His magic flowed from his fingers and into her body. It was strong enough to dissipate the poison but not heal the wounds.

"Rhea, you have to finish this. I don't have as much magic as you."

"No."

"Damn it! You aren't doing this. Do you hear me?"

He used what he could from the bandit's pack to clean her wounds. Once the bleeding stopped, he ran through the woods, gathering up what ingredients he would need for a salve to help speed up her healing.

Opening his pouch, he removed the small pestle and mortar, pressing in the flowers and weeds. He packed them into the wounds, cleaned them off, then sutured them up. Doubt crept in, that she may not survive.

"Please, stop," she begged as he bandaged her shoulder.

"You will live. I make you this promise, one day we will see the roses at your cottage together."

"Really?"

"I swear it on my own life."

Everything faded to black as she lost consciousness.

Argus found a cave to help keep Rhea dry as the drizzle continued. He carried her in and gently placed her on the pile of cloaks he collected from the dead bandits.

He gathered wood, lit a fire, and brought the horse in as well. It started raining harder as he returned with the remaining supplies.

Argus tended to Rhea, inspecting her wounds from time to time, only leaving to relieve himself, or to scout around to ensure no one else would ambush them. He set a few traps around the cave once the rain eased.

Rhea moaned and mumbled in her sleep, and fever overtook her when her stomach wound became infected. Argus used what magic he could, though it took everything he had to do so.

He collapsed beside her, pulling her to him, and praying to every deity he could name she would survive.

Chapter 4

The Cave

Rhea came to when Argus removed the bandage to check her shoulder. She glanced around, realizing they were in a cave, and the rain pattered on the roof.

"How long was I out?"

"Nearly a day and a half. You gave me a fright."

She winced when she sat up. "You tended to me?" Her gown was clean, and she'd been washed fairly recently.

"I did."

"Why did you say those things? Why did you have the key? What else did you lie about? Why are you able to lie?"

"Whoa, slow down. I know it's a lot to take in. First, you need to continue to rest. Since you refuse to use your own power, your healing is slow."

"I'm fine," she said, wincing in pain and clutching his hand. Her jaw clenched as she waited for it to ease. When it didn't, she knew she had no other choice. A bright light engulfed her, and within a few seconds, she completely healed. "Happy now?"

"Yes. Why didn't you do that right away?"

"I told you why." She let out a yawn. "I'm all right now, but exhausted."

"I found some rabbits earlier, so I have a stew simmering." He reached into his pack, then shoved something under the cloak beside her while she watched the flames.

"It smells good. I'm starving."

"You should be."

"Will you answer my questions now?"

"Where to begin? First, I do not have much magic, and I am able to lie, because I am only half-fae. My father hailed from the Wind Court and my mother a mortal from this realm."

"Are you serious?"

"Yes."

"Why are you doing this?"

He noted the hitch in her voice. "Because I don't have a choice."

"What do you mean?"

Instead of responding, he went to the fire, and scooped them out each a bowl of stew. He handed one to her.

"Careful, it's hot."

She took it and set it beside her. The rain outside pummeled down. Rhea stood and walked to the opening of the cave, close enough for the mist to spray her face. Argus appeared beside her.

"Don't worry. I'm not trying to escape." Her jaw ticked. "I already tried, but my magic hasn't recovered." She lifted up her palm to collect droplets of water before her hand fell to her side. "I just wanted to see the rain."

"Come, you need to eat and rest."

He wrapped his arm over her shoulder and guided her to the fire. Once settled in, she slowly ate, then set the empty bowl beside her.

Argus helped her lie down then covered her with his cloak. "You need a little more sleep before we continue."

Her eyelids drooped. Realization sank in. "What did you put in my stew?"

"It'll help you."

"You poisoned me?"

He laughed. "No, Princess. Medicated, not poisoned. Get a few more hours of sleep, and hopefully the rain will be gone by the time you wake up."

She glared at him as her mind drifted into a fog. Her jaw went slack, and she fell right to sleep. Argus adjusted the cloak around her, then stood and walked to the mouth of the cave.

Emotions swirled through him, some he understood but some scared him. He steeled himself, reminding himself she is his prisoner, nothing more. He would return her, receive his reward, and be on his merry way.

Why did the thought of handing her over to Mal make him a little sick to his stomach? Yes, he branded her. It's a common practice with royalty, to ensure the female remembered her place.

Argus watched Rhea as she slept by the light of the fire. Except, she was no ordinary female. She was the most beautiful one he'd ever seen. On top of that, she jumped in the way, getting injured while protecting him.

She only did it because she doesn't want to return to Mal, not because she cared for Argus. Right? At least, it's what he tried to tell himself.

He became lost in thought, and time slipped away. It grew darker as the storm raged on. When he knelt down to examine her once more, he checked his pocket watch, only to discover two hours had gone by.

The medicine should have worn off, and he would be able to wake her without any problems. He caressed her cheek with the back of his hand, seeing her at peace. Guilt ripped through him again, but he forced it down.

"Get up, we need to go." His voice was gruff.

Rhea slowly sat up. "Already? But it's still raining."

"It's easing. By the time we get everything packed, it will have stopped."

Rhea stood, wrapped the cloak around her, and slowly approached him. She gently grabbed his arm.

"Something's wrong, isn't it?"

He moved to jerk away but couldn't do it. Instead, he gripped her hand. In one swift move, he pulled her to him, his face only inches from her own.

"Argus," she breathed out, trembling under him.

Her mouth opened again to speak only to be cut off as his lips collided with hers. His hands gripped her back, the cloak falling from her, as she let herself be enveloped in his arms.

Argus stepped back. "I'm sorry. I—"

"I want this."

He cocked his head. "I beg your pardon?"

"I mean it. Because once you return me to the court, I will never know love or happiness. At least give me the pleasure to remember. Will you do this for me?"

"I won't be gentle," he threatened.

"I don't care. As long as I enjoy it, that's all I ask."

"Are you sure?"

"Please, give me what I've never known."

She unbuttoned her gown, and he watched it fall on top of the cloak. His breath sucked in when her corset went next. Unable to resist her, he swooped down, kissing her lips as he caressed her chest. His thumb swirled slowly over her peak.

As if he'd been struck, Argus staggered backward. "We can't do this. They will kill me if they find out."

"They won't."

"I can lie, you cannot."

"For starters, there is no way for them to prove if I am pure or not. Secondly, all I would tell them is it was a male I met in the mortal realm, which is the truth."

Argus debated for a moment. She slowly lowered her underwear before gently kicking it away. Her legs spread, and she teased herself with her fingers. His body stiffened as all thought flew from his mind.

He rushed to her, lifted her up, and took her to the fire. After gently placing her on his cloak, he stripped down. When he joined her, she caressed his jawline. He placed soft kisses along her neck while his hand teased between her thighs. She clenched in anticipation.

"Oh, no. We are taking this slow."

"But you said—"

"Forget what I said. I want you to enjoy every moment of this. So when we are no longer together, you will have the memory seared into your very flesh."

"I've already been branded," she murmured.

"I promise you, this kind will give you pleasant memories, not painful ones."

He lowered down and kissed the fine ginger hair between her legs. Her back arched when he teased her with his tongue. She gripped his hair, writhing and moaning as he brought her closer to the edge.

"Oh, gods!"

"No," he said sharply, his steely gaze driving into hers. "Say my name. Otherwise, I stop here."

She nodded in understanding. He resumed, his tongue drinking her while his fingers explored, eliciting another moan.

"Argus!"

"What do you want, Princess? Do you want me to continue this? Or are you ready for all of me?"

"I'm ready."

"Good girl."

He lifted up and slowly thrust himself inside her. She wrapped her legs around his waist, her breath hitching with each thrust, until he was fully seated within.

She held his shoulders, riding the waves of pleasure, and crying out his name. His hips continued to rise and fall in rhythm, each time sending her into pure bliss.

His lips devoured hers as he finished inside her. She eased back onto the cloak. Between magically healing herself and the physical exertion, her body and spirit were nearly spent.

Argus fixed her another bowl of stew. "Eat, Princess."

She ate without protesting and did not fail to hide her surprise when he took her again. Though exhausted, she would not refuse one moment of pleasure, not while it was so freely offered. They spent the afternoon into the evening in the throes of passion.

The day turned into night, and Rhea stepped out into the rain, gathering it and cleaning herself. She slipped back into the cave, dried by the fire, and dressed. Argus snored softly, and she climbed into his arms. She planted a kiss on his lips then lay beside him, ready for a full night of sleep.

Chapter 5

Trouble

Rhea awoke, smiling at Argus as she sat up. She yawned and stretched, only to discover the metal bindings were on her wrists once more. Her nostrils flared.

"Argus!"

He sat up with a start. "What's wrong?"

She held up her arms to him. "What is this?"

"Oh, come on, Princess. Did you think we would make *love* and suddenly I would change my mind?" The word love came out as though it were laced with poison.

"Of course not, but are these really necessary?"

"I know how powerful you are. You said yesterday you couldn't use your magic to escape. That's because I hid them by the cloaks, to prevent you after you healed yourself." He shook his head. "Never thought you'd use your magic on me, though."

"What are you talking about?"

"You clearly used some sort of seduction spell on me. Don't bother denying it."

"But I will, because I most certainly did not! Yesterday—"

"Was a mistake, plain and simple. Today, we will eat breakfast then continue on our way, since the rain has stopped. We only have about two days until we reach the faery gate."

"The other village—"

"We will not be stopping again. We've wasted enough time here. The next few days will be spent in silence. Otherwise, I will not hesitate to gag you. Do you understand?"

Though her eyes glistened with unshed tears, she kept her chin high. "I understand." Her expression revealed nothing of the heart breaking in her chest. She did not expect him to love her, but she thought perhaps he would come to care for her, even if only a little.

He went to his pack and took out what he needed to make breakfast. When he set the plate in front of her, she turned her nose up to it. She walked to the mouth of the cave.

The warmth of the morning sun added a pinch of color to her cheeks. She smiled, but it faded when she thought of returning to the Fire Court.

Two days. She had two days to convince him somehow to see reason. No matter what, she would not marry Mal. She assured herself.

Argus finished. He glanced at her full plate, debating, then took it to her. Before she could protest, he lifted his hand to silence her.

"Eat while I finish packing, or I'll bind your legs, too." Her chin and lips quivered, but he chose to ignore it as he shoved the meal in her face. "That was me asking nicely," he said as she reluctantly accepted it.

He returned to the dying fire, kicking dirt over it to ensure it went out. His knapsack lay by the cloaks. He gathered a few of them, rolled them up, and placed them inside. Satisfied they'd collected everything, he loaded it onto his back then grabbed hers.

"Here," he said, handing it to her.

As soon as she took it, he gripped her elbow and dragged her to the horse. After loading the saddle, they mounted, and began the next leg of their journey.

The forest slowly gave way into fields, then more trees. They passed a pond, stopped to rest a moment, then continued on the way. Rhea's stomach lurched at the thought of seeing her parents again.

What would they say to her? Would they be happy to see her? And Argus. How could she convince him she didn't use any magic on him? Most important of all, how would she convince him to leave her in the mortal realm?

Lost in her thoughts, she didn't hear his question. "I'm sorry. Did you say something?"

"I asked if you noticed how quiet it is."

She sat up and listened. "Trouble?"

"I think so."

He turned off the path and into the woods. They dismounted and stood by their horse, listening for any hoofbeats or other sounds of life. Rhea opened her mouth to ask, but he held up his hand. His head tilted south.

"That way," he whispered.

"How many?"

"I don't know."

"Will they—"

Argus was grabbed from behind and slammed onto the ground. Before Rhea could react, she was jerked backwards, with a gag forced into her mouth.

"I have the princess," a female's voice called out. "Take care of him."

"Yes, mi'lady," the male responded. Dressed in dark leathers, his cloak covered half his face. Rhea watched in fear as he removed his dagger. "I'll make it quick."

Argus jumped to his feet, unsheathing his own, and facing him. The female who held Rhea pulled her away from the fight. They walked for nearly a quarter of a mile before stopping. Rhea could finally see who abducted her.

Clearly a fae from the Earth Court, based on her attire. Her dark green leggings matched her tunic. Flowers and vines grew from her clothing, while her hair was as golden as the sun. She removed the gag.

"So, you're the little thing Mal wants so badly?"

"Who are you?"

"Mal and your father sent me to retrieve you. Instead, I'm going to gut you like a fish and leave you to rot."

"What? Why?"

"So Mal will marry me."

"You don't have to kill me. You win. Take him. I don't want to go back."

The fae was unable to hide her surprise. "I know you are not lying, but how can you say such things?"

"I don't love him, and I certainly don't want him."

"Regardless, if he found out you were alive, I would lose him. I can't take the chance."

"How will you avoid telling him you killed me when they ask where I am?"

"You died in the mortal realm. That will be the truth, wouldn't it?" she asked as she unsheathed her dagger.

Rhea backed away, but she charged at her. Rhea managed to turn at the last moment, and the blade went into her arm. She fell to the ground, clutching her elbow, and putting pressure on the wound. The fae made another attempt.

"Cassia, what are you doing?"

They looked to see her companion coming in between the trees. He glanced at Rhea before giving Cassia his attention.

She swore under her breath. "I thought you would take longer."

"For what? For you to kill her? That's not our plan."

"No, Eden, it's not your plan. Help me get this over with."

"We are not killing the princess. Have you lost your mind?"

"Where is Argus?" Rhea asked, straining her neck to see behind him.

The companion laughed. "Where do you think?" He turned serious as he faced Cassia. "We are taking her back, end of discussion."

Cassia lifted Rhea by her bindings, then swung her dagger down. Eden jumped at her and grabbed her arm, stopping the blade mere inches from Rhea's heart. Cassia rotated her arm and plunged the blade into his chest. Rhea screamed as he fell to the ground.

She broke free of Cassia's grip and ran as fast as she could. With her long legs and adrenaline pumping, she made fast strides. The forest gave way to a small clearing that ended with a cliff.

Rhea skidded to a stop, wobbling for a moment before catching herself. The ravine plunged hundreds of feet below. With Argus dead, and Cassia upon her any moment, she knew she didn't have a lot of options.

How easy it would be, to simply step off, and no longer exist. She would not be a pawn to her family nor a thing to be used by Mal. With resolve in her heart, she uttered a silent prayer before stepping forward.

Someone grabbed her by the shoulders and yanked her hard enough, she fell to the ground. She opened her eyes to see Cassia standing above her.

"Oh, no. You don't get off so easy! First, making me kill Eden, then having to chase you down. You will suffer before I end you."

She punched Rhea in the cheek. The next blow hit her in the ribs, and she cried out in pain. Cassia withdrew her blade then ran the tip across Rhea's face, from her chin to her forehead, causing a thin trail of blood to seep out.

"I could scar you. Mal would have no choice but to reject you. He would then be mine."

"Please, stop," Rhea begged, struggling to crawl away.

"This is so much—" Before she could finish, she was lifted off Rhea, and flung over the cliff.

Rhea kept her eyes squeezed shut, prepared for whatever horror awaited her next. Instead, a firm hand gripped her shoulder and pulled her tightly against his warm torso. His fingers caressed her back.

"I'm here. How badly are you hurt?"

She looked up to discover Argus holding her. "How are you still alive?" Blood dripped down his forehead but congealed around the wound higher up.

"I fooled him into believing I died, using a little magic to make it seem like it was much worse."

"I thought I lost you," she blurted out, unshed tears glistening.

He helped her stand and began to examine her. "Where all did she hurt you?"

The tears fell freely as she took a step back. "This is but a taste of what I have waiting for me when we return." She glanced at the cliff before meeting his gaze, only to see the worry drawn across his face. "I know what I must do."

"Stop," he commanded when she took another step.

"Why? It's not as though you care about me." She avoided his eyes as she spoke, looking at the ground instead.

"I can help you."

Her head jerked up with her mouth open in disbelief. "What?"

"I lied to you in the cave. I have a plan, but I can't tell you."

"Why not?"

"Because you are incapable of lying. They don't know I can. The ones who matter don't know, at least. Only a select few, the ones in my guild, do."

"Guild?"

He sighed. "I'm an assassin."

She shook her head, unable to grasp the words he spoke. "That's not true."

"It's a long story. What you need to know, I was sent because after a year using every spell they could conjure, no one else could locate you. They knew I have no magic, and I am highly skilled enough with my senses. It's why they asked me. Commanded, really. That's a story for another day. For now, you have to trust me."

"I can't. You are asking too much of me. If we return, and you hand me over to him—"

"I won't. I swear it." He swallowed hard, not sure he wanted the truth. "Why did you save me?"

"From the bandit?" she asked. He nodded in response. She took a moment to consider her next words. "Because, though you are my captor, I did not feel you deserved to die."

"Not because you would do anything to avoid returning to the Faeryland Kingdom? Or because you were more afraid of the bandit than you are of me?"

"While both of those are true, it is not what I was thinking when I watched him approach you. I genuinely feared for you, and I decided to do something about it. At least one of us can still have a life."

His heart sank when she faced the cliff once more. As if in a trance, she took another step away from him. She longed to be free of the future stretched ahead of her, one of unending pain. When she moved closer to the edge, Argus clasped her hand in his and pulled her against his chest.

Every emotion she fought burst out of her, and she sobbed into his cloak. He stroked her hair. "I mean it, Rhea. I have a plan. I'm going to help you."

She said nothing but let him continue to comfort her until the tears stopped. Argus gripped her chin, lifting her face until their eyes met.

"We need to clean up. Here." He laced his arm with hers and led her to a waterfall nearby.

They stripped down. As Rhea shimmied out of her gown, she let out a whimper of pain.

"What's wrong?" he asked, waiting patiently for an answer. When he received none, he gripped her shoulders, and examined her. "Rhea, tell me where she hurt you?"

"She cut my face, as you can see."

"And?"

"She punched me a few times and cut my arm, too."

"Promise me, if I remove the wrist cuffs so you can heal, you will not escape."

"Argus—"

"Promise me."

Her shoulders sagged. "I swear it, I won't escape." Her breath hitched. "It hurts."

He snatched up his pants, digging through until he found the pouch holding the keys. The cuffs were removed, then he tossed them aside.

After a few moments, Rhea encompassed herself with her magic, healing herself and Argus as well.

"I… I didn't expect this. Thank you," he said, as he placed the pouch in his pocket and let his pants fall to the ground.

He took her hand. Together, they entered the pool. He cupped water and washed the blood from her face. She returned the favor. His mouth opened in surprise when her lips met his.

She gripped his neck as she wrapped her legs around his waist. He held her tightly, returning her fire, as desire flowed between them.

He backed up to the edge of the pool, then gripped her hips, pulling himself into her. Her back arched, and she moaned at each thrust. Her head rolled back into the water, while her body slipped into the abyss of pleasure threatening to swallow her.

He lifted her to him, and she buried her face in his chest to stifle her scream as they reached the crescendo together. He held her in his arms as their hearts slowly resumed their normal beat.

Rhea swallowed her doubts before she faced him. "Please, tell me this isn't purely physical between us."

He cocked his head. "Why would you think that?"

She nervously bit her lower lip. "I don't know. It seems like… We… I mean—"

"Rhea, I am risking everything for you. Believe me when I tell you, what we have, is so much more than physical. Did I enjoy what we just did? Of course. But this here, holding you, being with you, means as much."

"Really?"

"My whole life has been planned out for me for as long as I could remember. I never envisioned a future with a mate, to be happy, and you. You are my happiness." He kissed her forehead. "Yes, it's true. This started as a job."

"For the guild?"

He shook his head as she moved away, leaning against the rocky wall of the pool. "No." Fear etched its way into his heart, fear that once he told her who he truly was, she would no longer want him. "Let's dry off and talk."

They stepped onto the small beach and dressed in silence. Rhea placed his cloak on the ground, then gestured for him to sit with her.

"I grew up with my father because my mother wasn't allowed to live with us in the fae realm. Only a few people know the truth about my lineage. My father and I were camping in the woods one night, and we were attacked. They killed him and took me, a seven-year-old child."

"They didn't hurt you?"

"I didn't say that." He gave her a sad smile. "They quickly realized I didn't have magic, and they were going to kill me, until they discovered I could lie. They used it to their advantage.

"If I wanted to eat or sleep, to not be beaten, I had no choice but to do what they said. Finally, I gave in. I told them I would do what they wanted. They told me to walk up to their target and pretend to be lost."

"Do I want to hear the rest of this story?"

"Probably not, but if we are going to be together, I want you to know who you are getting involved with."

"All right."

"While the target was distracted, they would strike." He couldn't bear to face her. His jaw clenched. "I never wanted to do it. There were times…" He took a shuddered breath. "There were times I would purposefully piss them off, so they would punish me. I felt I deserved it for what I did."

He flinched slightly when she caressed his cheek. "You were a child. You didn't have a choice."

"I grew up. Still, I pledged my loyalty and stayed with them."

"It was the only life you'd known."

"Rhea, I know what you're doing. Stop."

"What do you mean?"

"Don't make excuses for the things I've done."

She bit her lip but didn't say another word. He took her hand, kissing her palm, and planting soft kisses up her arm.

"I am grateful you want to, but I do not deserve such compassion. I did have one rule, one they never could get me to break."

"What rule?"

"No innocents, no females, no children. Until that night." He shook his head. "They found out a countess betrayed one of our own, so they sent me. They told me I didn't have a choice, my life or hers. I thought I could go, do my own reconnaissance, and prove her innocent."

"What did you find?"

"I was right. She'd been forced into it, after someone threatened to kill her younger sister. I refused to kill them, and my organization betrayed me in turn. They handed me over to the king for punishment, using me as their scapegoat."

"You were imprisoned?"

"Yes, and sentenced to death. They held me for nearly a year, each day threatening it would be my last. The torture…" When his eyes glistened, Rhea reached up to wipe away the unshed tears. "There were days I begged them to get it over with."

"I'm so sorry," she said softly.

"I deserved it for everything I've done in my past. My execution date drew near, and that's when your father came to see me." He patted his chest. "You asked about my mark? It's from a bargain. I would come to this realm, find you, and return you. In exchange, I would be pardoned for all past crimes, and given my freedom."

"That's what you meant when you said I couldn't pay you enough."

"Exactly. I want you to understand, I've never known love or compassion. My own father taught me to hunt and fish, to set a trap, but he was not a loving father. Then growing up the way I did…"

"Gods, no wonder you thought me a spoiled brat. You were absolutely right to think that."

"No, I shouldn't have said it. We both grew up to be used by those above us, instead of being loved and comforted. I'm sorry for the things I said before."

"Thank you."

"With you," pain stretched across his face with each word, "with you I feel like I am finally where I am supposed to be. I am at such peace. Even though I do not deserve it, I am taking it."

"What do you mean?"

"You, Rhea. I'm taking you for myself, even though I am a killer and a thief. I don't deserve you."

"How can you say that?"

"You are fire, blazing a trail of love and beauty everywhere you touch. Because of this, you are memorable. I am wind. No, I'm barely a breeze. A fleeting moment easily forgotten. I am nothing."

"Argus—"

He gripped her hand as though he would float away if he let go. "Even so, I have never wanted anything more than I do right now, to have you in my life. If you'll have me, I am yours."

"Yes." She kissed him again, caressing his chest as her tongue explored his mouth. "I want you, too. More than anything. There is one thing you are wrong about, though."

"Oh?"

"You aren't nothing. I love you, Argus, and you are everything to me."

His breath shuddered as he tore his gaze away. "But the things I've done—"

"You've more than paid for them. They are in the past. I am your future."

He smiled at her words before taking her again.

Chapter 6

Trust Me

Rhea gripped the warm mug and leaned towards the fire. She tried to argue when Argus insisted on putting the wrist cuffs on, but he reminded her there could be other fae around, trying to find her. He told her they needed to keep up the appearance of her as his prisoner.

Argus joined her a moment later to remove the skillet from the heat. They split the eggs and bread.

"How much farther until we arrive at the faery portal?"

"A day and a half. We have plenty of supplies. Especially since I helped myself to Cassia's rations."

Rhea laughed. "Ah, so that's where the peppermint tea came from."

He finished his breakfast and stood without answering. After checking their bags were packed on the horse's saddle, he turned to find Rhea before him.

She pressed herself into him, holding him tightly.

"Ready to go again so soon?"

She giggled. The sound was music to his heart, the sound of life and love. He smiled at her before kissing her fiercely.

"Just another minute," he said.

"I need longer than that."

His face reddened as he placed her on her feet. "I meant, another minute until we will be leaving." He tsked at her. "Very inappropriate, especially for a princess."

"What is your obsession with that?" she asked with a small laugh, only to turn serious at the dour expression on his face. "I'm sorry. What did I say?"

"It's nothing. Let's make sure we have everything before we head out."

She checked her bag, but her mind wondered what she could've said that offended him. She would find out once they were on the horse, and he couldn't evade her questions so easily.

Dread filled her at the thought of approaching the faery gate, but she would trust him. Her heart told him he was being honest, and she would have faith.

Argus lifted her onto the steed then jumped up behind her. She loved his possessiveness, with his arm wrapped tightly around her stomach. Her hand rested above his elbow, caressing him gently as they began to move.

"I'm sorry about what I said."

"Don't worry about it."

His rough voice gave her pause, and she decided to let it go for the time being. "Of course."

After three hours of riding, the trail opened from the woods into a field full of purple and pink flowers. Rhea's breath sucked in at the sight. She smiled at Argus with a hopeful expression plastered on her face.

"You want to stop here for lunch, don't you?" He chuckled when she nodded in response. He opened his pocket watch. "Well, it's only ten-thirty. We may have to work up an appetite."

"For you, I'm always hungry."

He dismounted first, pulling his cloak off, and spreading it on the flattest surface he could find. Next, he lifted her from the saddle. They sat together, and she kissed him tenderly.

"There's something we need to discuss," he said as he leaned away from her.

"What about?"

"Returning you to the kingdom." He gripped her wrist softly. "You will have to be chained when we arrive. They have to believe you are my prisoner, dragged there against your will. If for even a moment they suspect anything, everything could fall apart."

"I don't understand."

He lowered her arm before looking at her. "I know you must be tired of hearing this, but please trust me. Whatever I say or tell you to do, you have to believe it is for us. No matter what. Can you do that?"

"I guess I don't have a choice," she snapped as she jumped to her feet. "You won't tell me anything!"

"I can't," he reminded her as he joined her. "You know why not. If they use magic or torture to make you speak, the plan will never work. It's not that I don't trust you, Princess. It's them I have to worry about."

"Why not make a bargain with me, so I can't speak about this, no matter what?"

"Do you think I hadn't considered that? You said the night you met Mal, he stripped you down to examine you. What if they did that again?" He kissed her forehead. "They could torture you for hours to try and find out why you have a mark, and I can't bear the thought of it."

"It still hurts you won't tell me."

"Then let me help you how I can." His lips nuzzled her neck while his hand caressed her chest.

Part of her wanted to pull away, to tell him no, only if he'll tell her the whole plan. Except, everywhere he touched scorched her, bringing every bit of her desire to life. She couldn't ignore it, no matter how hard she tried.

She gave in, grabbing him to her, kissing him as her hand teased along his waistline. He lowered her to the ground and undressed her. His fingers stroked between her thighs when she began to unbutton his shirt. She's trying to undo the last button when her hips rise.

"Argus—"

"That's right, Princess. I'm the only one for you."

"But I'm going to…" Her words died in her throat when he removed his hand.

She glanced at him, lust and aching need written across her face. A yelp escaped her mouth when he grabbed her hips, lifted her legs over his shoulders, and began to devour her. Her eyes rolled back as she trembled.

"Oh, Argus!" she cried out.

He continued his assault, each lash of his tongue sending waves of overwhelming pleasure through her. Her body quivered, nothing more than a trembling leaf fighting the wind. Each touch fanned her desire, and she couldn't so much as think as she finished, losing count of each wave.

"I can't," she said as the last one consumed her whole. Her hips jerked, and she screamed in a mix of pain with pleasure as his tongue penetrated her.

He pulled back and gently lowered her onto the cloak. Her chest heaved with every breath, as a slight sheen of sweat highlighted her face.

"What about you?" she rasped out.

"No, Princess. I wanted this to be about you."

While she rested for a few minutes, he decided to start lunch. He lit a small fire and heated up stew while she slipped into her dress. She sat beside him while he stirred.

"It's a wonder I've never met you before, since my father does a lot of business with the Wind Court. Or is the guild located somewhere else?"

He swallowed hard. "You really don't remember me."

"What? What do you mean?"

His attention went back to the meal, as he removed bread and cheese from his pack to accompany it. "Here, eat this. The stew will be ready shortly."

"Have we met before?" she asked as she took the plate from him.

"You're two hundred and thirteen, right?"

"Yes, why?"

"I'm two hundred and fifteen. Do you remember your father's coronation? You were about five then."

"Vaguely."

"You were in a pink dress, and your mother did your hair with turquoise ribbons."

"How could you possibly know what I wore?"

"Because my father and I stood directly behind you, until you went up to the platform to sit with your family."

She shook her head. "I'm sorry. I don't remember you at all."

"Well, I don't have a head full of red hair, either."

"Lots of girls in the Fire Court have red hair."

"Not as fiery as yours. But what really made you stand out? The diamond tiara you wore."

"Hence your obsession with calling me princess?"

He poured them each a bowl. Softly blowing to cool his down, he kept his gaze low. "Yes."

"What's wrong?"

"It's nothing."

"Argus, please. Open up to me."

He set the bowl beside him. "It was that night my father and I were ambushed."

She reached for him, but he stood and walked to the horse. Argus checked to be sure her bag was secure, keeping his back to her. She couldn't take it any longer, and she went to him.

"I'm sorry."

With one arm, he pulled her to him and buried his face in the crook of her neck. For over two hundred years, he never shed a tear for his father. Until now.

"Why have we stopped?" Rhea asked as she scanned the area around them.

Argus helped her dismount. "Close your eyes." He smiled when she cocked her head at him. "What do I always say?"

"Trust you."

"Exactly."

"Fine." With reluctance, she did as he asked.

He removed his pack and carried it to the pond nearby. After laying out his cloak and cheese with bread, he returned to her. He led her to the spot he set up.

"Open them."

"What is this?" she asked, smiling at him.

"We will return to the kingdom tomorrow. I'm being selfish and taking a little more time with you before everything explodes."

She laughed softly. "Hey, how am I supposed to have faith in your plan if you don't even have it yourself?"

"I do have a solid plan, but there are a lot of variables. Even so, I need this time with you. If you tell me you don't need it, too—"

His words were cut off when she kissed him. She began to unbutton her gown, but he took her hand. Then he proceeded to undress her. He removed her restraints before helping her onto the cloak.

She smiled as he stripped out of his clothing before joining her. "Hmm, and what are we doing out here?"

"I mean, if you have to ask…"

She blushed. "No, I mean, what do you want from me?"

"I want everything. Why are you still so shy with me? I have seen and tasted every inch of you."

Her face only reddened more. "I know, but all of this seems so sudden. I haven't known you a week, yet in my heart, it's as though I've known you my entire life."

"I feel the same way."

He kissed her softly as his hand explored her chest and stomach. When his fingers grazed her navel, her breath sucked in. Gooseflesh crept over her while his tongue opened her lips and invaded her mouth.

In one subtle move, he pulled her down, so her back landed on the cloak. He leaned over her as her legs wrapped around his waist.

"Please," she begged as she gripped his arms. "I need you badly."

"I need you, Princess. I need you begging for me like this. I need your mouth on mine. I need every piece of you."

He entered her slowly, determined he would not hurt her. When she whimpered, he froze in place.

"What's wrong."

"I want you inside me," she said as her whimper turned into a moan.

Unable to hold back any longer, he lunged into her, his body fully entangled with hers. Sweat began to bead on her forehead as she met every thrust with the same enthusiasm he did. He kissed her again, his fingers teasing her softest spot as he continued to slam into her.

Her mouth opened to scream, but the sound died in her throat as his lips consumed hers. When he could hold back no longer, filling her, she trembled under him as she came undone.

Slowly, he lowered her to the cloak before lying beside her. Her eyes remained closed, and for a moment, he worried he hurt her somehow. That is, until she climbed on top of him, planting kisses on his jawline as his hand caressed her back.

"How did that feel?"

"Gods, it was fantastic."

He laughed in response. "We'll get some rest, eat a late supper, then head out at midnight."

"Oh, right. I forgot, if we leave here at night, we'll arrive there at daytime."

He winked. "Exactly. Though, I've heard they are improving the magic, so one day, there won't be a difference in travel time."

"Hmm, that would be nice."

She snuggled into his arms, her breathing steady, and he realized for the first time in his life, there was someone who trusted him. She trusted him with her life and her safety. Whatever he asked or demanded, she would gladly give him without question. He kissed her forehead, continuing to hold her tight, and knowing tomorrow was the day he would betray her.

Chapter 7

The Faeryland Kingdom

They approached the faery gate. The blue rings shone brightly under the cloudy night sky. She collected herself before meeting his gaze. "I trust you, you know I do. Still, I'm frightened."

"I know you are. It's going to be all right. Whatever happens, remember that."

He kissed her softly before lacing her arm with his, then they walked into the rings. A flash of light, and they were back in the Faeryland Kingdom. She took in her surroundings.

"It hasn't changed much since I left."

"We can—"

"Halt!"

Two royal guards approached. Their silver armor shone with green accents. Vines with leaves wove around their arms and legs.

"Do you not recognize the princess?" Argus asked.

The men exchanged a glance before looking at her. "Of course we do. We were instructed to wait here for your return." They each offered Rhea a bow.

"I don't understand. You are from the Earth Court!" she cried out.

"The war has ended," the shorter of the two explained. "About four months ago, an understanding was brought about. Another two months later, they signed a treaty."

Rhea sighed in relief. "So I am no longer betrothed to Mal?"

The guard shifted on his feet. "Apologies, Your Highness, but that is how the treaty came to be."

"What?"

"Your father threatened Mal. He said when you were returned, he would withhold you from him if he continued with the war."

Tears glistened in her eyes. "You can't be serious."

Argus signaled for the guards to give them privacy. As soon as they were out of earshot, he gripped her chin, his gaze locking with hers.

"Listen to me. This changes nothing. We came here knowing you were betrothed to him, right? My plan will work. Stay with me, Princess."

Rhea took a deep breath. "I will."

"That's my girl. We only have to keep up this façade a short while longer. Can you do this?"

"I can. I will do whatever I must, not only to free myself of Mal, but to be with you."

"Now, play along." He stood up straight and jerked her forward. "Enough backtalk, Princess. Your father is waiting for you."

No words were spoken as they entered the carriage and started the journey to the Fire Court. Rhea's heart thudded heavily in her chest the entire ride. Argus could see her distress. However, one of the guards rode with them, so Argus couldn't reassure her the way he wanted to.

They arrived at the palace. Argus helped Rhea disembark. He kept a firm grip on her arm as they were led inside. To see fae from every court talking, eating, mingling in the same space, Rhea couldn't believe it.

"Is this real?" she asked Argus.

"Apparently."

They walked into the massive throne room. The granite walls and marble columns were off-white, and the floors a dark grey. Save the king, queen, and a handful of guards, there were no spectators. Relief washed over Rhea because Mal was nowhere to be found.

"Our daughter has returned," the king said as he stood. He approached Rhea before turning to Argus. "You have upheld your end."

"Yes, Your Majesty."

"So, daughter, anything you have to say for yourself?"

"Nothing has changed," she said as her posture stiffened. "I will not marry Mal."

"You have no choice. The matter has already been decided."

"Ah, my blushing bride has been returned to me!"

Rhea tensed against Argus. Sweat gathered at the nape of his neck as bile threatened to rise in his throat. He knew what would happen next.

Mal approached them both and slammed his palm onto Argus's shoulder. "Well, Your Majesty, I told you my nephew would be perfect for this job."

His green eyes sparkled as he studied Rhea. At nearly a foot taller than her, everything about him seemed threatening to her. She noted his light brown hair had been recently cut, and she knew other women saw him as handsome. After the things he said and did to her, she would never see him that way.

When his gaze raked over her, taking her in, Rhea lost what little color she had. Her eyes went as wide as saucers, and she looked at Argus with utter disbelief etched across her face.

"Tell me it's not true," she whispered. "He's not really your uncle, is he?"

"Silence," Argus commanded. He turned to the king. "Before I hand her over, there is the matter of payment to be addressed."

"Of course. First, Argus, you are free of our bargain."

Argus gripped his chest momentarily, then stood up straight, attempting to keep a cool demeanor.

"What exactly was your bargain?" Rhea asked Argus.

The king responded instead. "He was given thirty days to find you and bring you here, or he would die."

"What?"

"His heart would give out if he failed."

Rhea couldn't believe what she heard. She shook her head as a single tear slid down her cheek. "No," she murmured.

"Secondly," Tristan continued as he removed a piece of parchment from his pocket, "is your pardon. This states you are pardoned of any and all previous crimes." The king pulled it out of reach when Argus grasped at it. "This is a fresh start, and it does not protect you from any future decisions you may make."

"I understand," Argus said as he took it. "Thank you, Your Majesty."

Rhea braced herself, waiting for the moment he would enact his plan. She kept her face neutral, though her heart thudded in her ribcage. Argus smirked at her.

"Now, Princess, this has been fun. But it's time for me to be on my way."

Rhea could only blink in response, unsure of what he meant or what he would do next.

"Wait," Mal said as he stepped forward. "Our wedding is tomorrow. After all the trouble you went through, I insist you attend."

"I would be honored, but I have nowhere to stay."

"We will arrange guest chambers for you," the king said. "For tonight only."

"That is gracious, Your Majesty. Very well, I accept." Argus gave a bow and turned to leave.

"Argus." Rhea stepped forward when a guard grabbed her arm.

He kept his head turned away. "Trust me, Princess. Tomorrow you get what you deserve." His voice chilled her to the bone.

No love or joy were in his eyes when he finally looked at her, before spinning on his heel. Her breath hitched, her vision faded, and she lost consciousness as soon as the door slammed shut behind him.

"Princess Wisteria, how do you feel?"

A handmaid hovered over Rhea. She glanced around and discovered she was in her bedroom. "I haven't been in here for a year," she murmured as she slowly sat up. "What happened?"

"They said you fainted in the throne room. My magic detected no illnesses or wounds."

"I became overwhelmed," Rhea admitted. "I never intended to return here."

"I am Lyrie. I have been commanded by your father to take care of you until the ceremony, which is tomorrow morning at ten o'clock."

Rhea clutched the blanket to her chest. "I will not marry him."

Lyrie gave her a sympathetic smile. "Either way, I cannot refuse my king. Now, let's get you cleaned up and into a proper gown."

Hiding under the covers appealed to Rhea, but she pushed the childish thoughts away as she stood. "Very well." She knew Lyrie could not be held at fault. "I would like a bath, if it's not too much trouble." She looked down to see they removed the chain, but the wrist cuffs remained.

"I'll see to it now," Lyrie said. She went into the washroom.

Rhea rushed to the door, expecting to find it locked. Instead, she nearly fell backward when it opened for her. She clutched the edge of it to keep her balance.

"Do you need something, Your Highness?"

She raised her head, only to see four guards at their post, protecting her and imprisoning her at the same time. "Um, when will food be here?" she managed to squeak out.

"Your father has asked for you to join him and the queen this evening. We will escort you there in an hour."

"Thank you."

Rhea shut the door and turned to find Lyrie eyeing her suspiciously. "Is everything all right, mi'lady?"

She forced a smile. "I am going to dinner with my parents in an hour."

"Of course. Come, your bath should be ready."

Rhea followed her in and reluctantly stripped down, unsure around this stranger. She thought back to her conversation with Argus, regarding making a bargain. He was right. If there was a noticeable mark on her, her handmaid might've informed the king.

"Mi'lady, are you all right?"

Rhea finished undressing and slid into the tub. The hot water soothed her tense muscles, while the rosewater scent calmed her senses. Lyrie offered her a glass of tea or wine.

"Tea, please."

"Yes, mi'lady." Lyrie stepped out to see to it.

Rhea tried to relax, but her mind kept going to the scene in the throne room. Argus was unrecognizable when he spoke to her at the end, his voice and eyes so dead to the world. She assured herself it was a façade, that he played a part for the plan he'd concocted. Perhaps he would break her out tonight.

If she could make it through dinner then wait for him, everything would be all right. Surely it's what he intended, right? Although, he promised her he wouldn't hand her over to her father or Mal, and he already broke it. Doubt seeped into her heart, and though she tried to fight it down, the tears fell fast.

"Mi'lady, are you hurt?" Lyrie asked, holding the teacup and saucer in the palm of her hand.

"I'm not injured," Rhea responded. "I'm a little emotional at the moment." It was the truth.

"Here, this will help."

Rhea drank the tea slowly, enjoying the peppermint flavor with each sip. When she finished, she handed the empty cup to Lyrie then drained the tub. Rhea dried off before going to her closet.

A pastel blue gown caught her eye. After dressing, she sat on the bed to put her shoes on when Lyrie approached her.

"Mi'lady, what are you doing?"

"I'm… getting ready."

"Like that?"

"Is something wrong with my gown?"

Lyrie waved her hand. "Why did you not do that and dress yourself?"

"My wrist cuffs, they suppress my magic."

"Of course. It's why they removed them so I could examine you. My apologies."

Rhea laughed softly, hoping to hide her embarrassment. "Plus, where I lived in the mortal realm, I had to limit my magic usage. Most of it was spent trying to hide myself. I became accustomed to dressing like this as well."

"I see. Are you ready to go to dinner?"

Of course not, but Rhea didn't have a choice. "Lead the way."

She followed Lyrie into the corridor, where the guards surrounded them, then led them to the dining room. The king and queen stood when the guards parted, exposing Rhea. Despite so many people around her, she'd never felt so alone. Lyrie gave her a sympathetic smile before she left.

Rhea gave a small bow before joining her parents. Her mother took her hand.

"I've missed you."

"I doubt it," Rhea said as she pulled away, keeping emotion out of her voice as best she could. She looked at her father. "Why am I here?"

"Don't be rude to your mother," he scolded. "You know she means it. She did miss you. She cried when we discovered you were gone."

Rhea's expression softened, if only a little. "I told you both, I will not marry Mal. You refused to listen and left me no choice."

"Do you have any idea what could've happened?" Tristan asked. "Or do you even care? What if we were still at war?"

"I didn't start the war!" Rhea slumped in her chair, realizing it would do no good to rehash everything with her parents. Before she could say another word, Tristan's anger overflowed.

"No, but you could've put a stop to it," he bellowed. The servants approaching with their meals paused, and Rhea's mother placed her hand on Tristan's arm. "What were you thinking?"

"Please," her mother tried.

"He branded me!" Rhea screeched in return.

"It is not uncommon for a husband to do so to his bride," Tristan said while gesturing for their meals.

"We aren't married," Rhea reminded him. "He had no right to touch me that way. Not that either of you care."

"We do care, really," her father said. "However, you are but one fae. I have an entire realm to take care of. I was trying to save lives. This great war has lasted centuries longer than it needed to."

Rhea's eyes narrowed. "I know it's what you believe, but I assure you, there were other ways to go about it. I offered to fight—"

"You are our only child, and you know how difficult it is for our people to conceive. We would not risk losing you. At least with marriage, you are alive and able to give us an heir."

"That's all I've ever been to you. Your precious princess, to show off, to use how you see fit."

"That's not true."

"My entire life, you have told me how to dress, where to go, who to converse with or dine with. I have been nothing but a pawn in your game."

"Wisteria, you don't—"

"That is no longer my name. I go by Rhea now."

Her mother's shoulders sagged as the look of defeat crept over her face. "Please, we have to work together."

"I am telling you both right now. If you force me to go through with the binding ceremony tomorrow, I will not be around to see the sunset."

"Mal wouldn't kill you. He knows as soon as the ceremony is complete, your lives are tied together. He wouldn't risk that to himself."

"I didn't say he would be the one who kills me."

Her mother gasped. "Surely, you exaggerate. It's not so bad. Our marriage was arranged, and you see how happy we are together." As if to make her point, she clasped Tristan's hand and smiled at him.

"You were lucky. Love and marriage rarely go together within the higher rankings. I want to marry for love. Why do you refuse to see that?"

"We don't refuse to see it, but war is still a possibility. If you do not marry Mal, he has the power to destroy the treaty. He would destroy the peace we have worked so hard to rebuild. Give him a chance," Tristan said, attempting to keep a steady tone as he did so.

Rhea stood and stepped back. "I am done with this conversation."

"Wisteria, please," her mother begged, but Rhea turned and fled the scene.

She returned to her room, sinking to the floor after the door shut behind her. The tears formed, but she refused to waste any more on her parents or her situation. She wiped them away, when a knock at the door startled her.

"Go away!" she cried out, not caring whether it was her mother or father on the other side.

The door opened, and she gasped when Mal entered. "That is not how one speaks to her husband."

"Lucky for me, you and I aren't married."

The door slammed behind him, and he gripped her neck in his hand. "Listen here. I branded you, claimed you, and tomorrow, I will get to enjoy everything about you. There isn't a single thing you can do."

"Please," she tried, her breathing coming in shallow gasps. "You're hurting me."

He released her throat only to grip her chin. Leaning down, his face inches from hers, he smiled. "As if anything you say can stop that. I will hurt you, heal you, then hurt you all over again. You will never be able to speak of the things I do, either."

"What do you mean?"

He spread out his fingers and jerked his hand to her, but nothing happened. "What the hell?"

"Oh."

"What?" he demanded.

She held up her arms. "My bindings are pure iron."

"I see. That's why I can't—" He stopped speaking as his head tilted. "Tomorrow. We have to do something."

"What do you mean?" she asked, though she was certain he was not speaking to her.

"I have to go."

As soon as he left, she collapsed onto her bed. She ran her fingers over her neck and had just collected herself when there came another knock.

"I am in no mood for company," she declared, grateful her voice came out steady.

"It is urgent I see you, mi'lady."

Rhea didn't recognize the female's voice. She opened the door, only to see Argus and a priestess. He was arguing with her guards.

"Do you dare defy your king?" Argus asked. "He commanded the priestess and I attend to his daughter before the ceremony tomorrow." His tone was firm and authoritative as he spoke.

The head guard looked uneasy but realized there was no choice. "You may go in."

Argus scoffed before following the priestess into Rhea's chambers. As soon as the door shut, he glanced around the room, taking in the size of it and the décor before giving Rhea his attention.

"What are you doing here?" she asked.

"I told you to trust me. Do you not?"

Her head lowered down as her hands clasped together. "I did until you handed me over to them."

"I had to," he shot back. "How many times do I need to remind you, I can lie while you cannot. If they questioned you—"

"I know, but how can I trust you now?"

Argus started to answer until he saw the marks. "What happened?"

She turned away. "I… I don't want to talk about it."

"It was Mal, wasn't it?"

She broke down, before telling him everything that had transpired.

"Rhea, I am so sorry." He reached for her, but she recoiled from his touch. "If you won't give me your trust, I ask you give it to her."

The priestess stepped forward. "Your Highness, Argus told me everything. I am here to see you are not bound to Mal tomorrow."

"What do you mean? What are you going to do?"

Argus held up a key. "No one took this from me when I returned you, as I figured they would forget. Now, we have to act quickly."

Rhea straightened her veil as Lyrie applied the final touches to her hair.

"You look lovely, Your Highness."

"Thank you."

The pale pink chiffon gown flowed as she walked to the door. While the V-neck was a little lower than Rhea would've preferred, the lace sleeves and roses on the bodice appealed to her. It clung to her, accentuating her hips and waist while the skirt billowed with each step.

Rhea followed her from the small changing room and to the chapel. She was surprised to see Tristan waiting for her at the entrance. Did he want to walk her down the aisle?

When she approached him, he lifted a key. "We need to remove your wrist cuffs, so they don't interfere with the binding ceremony." He scowled at her smile. Without another word, he removed the cuffs then slipped an iron ring onto her right-hand middle finger.

"What is that?" she asked, examining the simple band.

"It will suppress your magic without interfering with the ceremony. We came up with it last night."

"We?"

"Your future husband and me. It is also enchanted so the wearer is unable to remove it."

Rhea realized even thinking about taking the ring off caused a burning sensation where it rested. Her brow furrowed, but she let it go for the time being. Lyrie approached Rhea and handed her a bouquet of pale pink roses.

"For you, mi'lady."

"Thank you."

Rhea turned to her father. "Are you walking me down the aisle?"

He chuckled at her question. "I have to be sure you don't run away again."

Her face contorted for a moment, the pain apparent, before she resumed a cool visage. The music began as soon as the massive doors opened. The audience stood, watching in silent reverence. She kept her head high as they made their way to the altar.

Standing before the priestess, her father took her hand and placed it into Mal's. Rhea's stomach did a flip at his touch. They turned to face the priestess, and everyone sat down.

"We are gathered here today to join Grand Earl Mal and Princess Wisteria in our traditional binding ceremony." A bell rang, and she held up a silver ribbon. "Let us begin."

She wrapped the ribbon around Mal and Rhea's wrists, then stepped back and waited. After a moment, murmurs broke out in the audience.

"Is something the matter?" Rhea asked.

The priestess rearranged the ribbon but still nothing happened. "It's… The ribbon should be shimmering with magic," she said softly, almost to herself.

The king quickly approached. He used his body to shield the view of the audience while he removed Rhea's ring. He returned to his seat without another word.

A few minutes went by, but the ribbon still remained the same. Clearly confused, the priestess shook her head, unsure of what to do next.

"It's because she is already bound to a fae."

Everyone turned to see Argus at the entrance of the chapel. Dressed in black pants with a dark blue tunic shirt, trimmed in gold, Rhea couldn't believe how handsome he looked. He took a few steps towards the altar when royal guards stopped him.

"What do you mean?" Mal demanded. "She is going to be bound to me!"

"Did you really think I would let you have my mate?"

At the last word, Rhea's heart swelled. She gasped softly, attempting to keep her feelings in check. Mal glanced at Rhea before returning his attention to Argus.

"I don't understand."

"She is mine," Argus proclaimed. "We held our binding ceremony last night."

"Impossible!" Tristan declared, jumping to his feet and rushing to the priestess. "Are you responsible?"

While he was distracted, Rhea quickly removed the ring from his pocket and hid it in her bouquet. The priestess trembled before him.

"No, Your Majesty."

"I am." The fae from the night before stood and faced him.

The king walked to her and jabbed his index finger in her face. "Why would you do such a thing?"

"Because it is not my place to deny true love."

The king scoffed. "I beg your pardon?"

She stripped out of her cloak to reveal her white faery wings. "I am Alyssa, and I am a follower of Cupid. Argus knew this and sought me out. He asked for the ceremony, after he told me it was true love."

Tristan spun on his heel to face Argus. "How can you possibly believe in such a thing? It's a myth! I'm not saying there isn't love among our kind, but true love does not exist."

Argus shoved through the guards and continued down the aisle. "In our case, that's what it is. Alyssa didn't believe me, either. Not at first. She confirmed it before she would bind us together."

He stood close to Rhea, and she wanted desperately to reach out to him, to hold his hand, to touch him. Without meaning to, she stepped away from Mal, causing the ribbon to fall to the floor.

Gasps and murmurs of outrage exploded. The king quickly silenced the crowd. "He used some sort of magic on her!"

Rhea snorted. "He most certainly did not. The only one who has hurt me against my will is Mal." She lifted her hair to show the mark on the back of her neck. "He branded me when we first met. And you let him." She then brought her hands together, clasping the bouquet tightly.

"Wisteria, please be reasonable," her father pled.

"You had your chance." She looked at Mal. "I do not belong to you."

"My mark on you confirms otherwise."

Rhea smiled. "I hoped you would say that."

"What do you mean?"

"It's your family crest, isn't it?"

"Well, yes, but what has that to do with—"

"It's also the family crest for your nephew. I knew I recognized it on his flask when he offered me water."

His eyes went wide. "Son of a…" His voice trailed off. "You used our blood to go against me!" he screeched at Argus.

"You did that to yourself," he responded. "You tried taking what doesn't belong to you. We are not to mark our mate until *after* we are bound, and not everyone continues this archaic tradition. You broke the rules."

Mal gripped Rhea's wrist and yanked her to him. "She is mine!"

"Big mistake." Rhea spun and dropped the bouquet. Producing the ring in her cupped palm, she enchanted it. Mal jerked for a moment then stared at his hand in disbelief, only to see it on his index finger.

"What are you doing?"

"Using your ring for its intended purpose. It will suppress your power, rendering you useless. You are no longer a threat."

She raised her hands and sent flames after his clothing. They did not harm his skin or hair, only leaving him naked in front of the audience. Shock washed over him at first. Then he rushed from the room to escape their laughter.

Argus went to Rhea, enveloping her in his embrace, and kissing her fiercely. "I meant what I said last night. I am grateful to be bound to you. I want no one else."

"Enough!" Tristan cried out. "What a nightmare. Everyone else, leave now!" The crowd stood and filed from the chapel. The king massaged his brow before facing the priestess. "There is no way to undo a binding ceremony, is there?"

She vehemently shook her head. "It has never been attempted, as it is meant to be permanent."

"Then I command you to try it now."

Alyssa's mouth opened to protest, but Rhea beat her to it. Fire again raced in her hands. "You have taken enough from me. You have denied me love and kindness my entire life. I will not be used anymore!"

"You are a princess. It comes with the territory."

"Then I deny my blood and family, and I abdicate any right to the throne. I am no longer your daughter."

"Wait, you can't—"

Argus watched as a green light shimmered around Rhea and her father. Tristan's skin went pallid as he realized what she'd done.

"You severed all familial ties?"

"Yes. I should've done it sooner, but I held onto hope that one day you might come to love me."

"If that's how you want it. This goes both ways. You are hereby banished from all fae courts. I will also take your magic!"

He whispered furiously then launched a bright red light at them both. Argus stood beside Rhea, clutching her hand, as the king's spell continued. The light dissipated, and Rhea collapsed into Argus's arms.

"Guards, take them to the faery gate."

"Please, don't banish her."

Rhea couldn't hide her surprise at her mother's words. Argus helped her stand straight as she faced her. "You have said nothing while everything transpired. What's done is done. You had your chance to speak on my behalf. Goodbye, Mother."

Chapter 8

Home

Rhea and Argus arrived in the mortal realm. He held her tightly. "Are you all right?" he asked, the concern thick in his voice.

"I'm fine. How do you feel?"

"The same."

She smiled. "We need to rest now."

"Where will we go?"

Rhea held him to her and vaolmersed them to her cottage. Argus said nothing as she went to her pantry. She set out some cheese and dried meat.

"Are you hungry?" She looked up when he didn't respond. "Argus?"

"How the hell did you do that? I thought he took our power."

She laughed as she sliced up the aged cheddar. "No, he only thought he did. I knew what he would do, so I put a ward around us both. His spell thought it drained our magic, but it took the ward instead. I pretended to be exhausted so he would believe it worked."

"Gods, you are incredible!" He rushed to her and kissed her, slowly taking the knife and setting it down. "Don't need this at my throat, do I?" He lifted her onto the counter, standing between her legs as his tongue explored her mouth.

"What now?" she asked when he backed away for air.

"I have a plan."

"Hmm, another plan. Do I trust you?"

He feigned hurt. "Let's eat. You get some rest, and I will return in a day or so."

"You have to leave?"

"I do," he said, lifting her hand and kissing her palm.

"Why can't I come with you?"

"Because I want to surprise you. Call it a wedding present."

"Very well." Her tone remained steady but light sparkled in her eyes. Argus smiled at the sight.

After they ate, he tucked her into bed. "Believe me, I want to climb in there with you and hold you while we sleep. Soon enough, I promise." He placed a gentle kiss above her brow. "I'll see you in a few days."

"What should I do while you're gone?"

"Pack your belongings."

"Where are we going?"

He only smiled before he left.

Rhea spent the next two days packing and tidying around the cottage. She was thrilled when Argus returned in time for lunch.

"After we eat, we'll hit the road."

"So soon?" she asked, taking a sip of her tea.

"It's for the best, I promise."

"What do you mean?"

"I'm afraid the longer you stay here, the harder it will be to say goodbye. I assure you, where we are going, you and I will be happy."

She sighed but didn't argue. While he washed dishes, she went into town to bid farewell. She did the best she could to keep her emotions in check, until Sylvan hugged her. She thanked him for everything he'd done for her and promised she would be back to visit one day.

When she returned home, Argus had everything loaded up in the cart he borrowed. They checked once more to be sure they hadn't forgotten anything before heading for their new destination.

Rhea asked questions about where they were going, but he only smiled at her. They traveled for several hours, stopping to rest before continuing. She nodded off, and when she came to, they were approaching a small village.

"Where are we?"

"This is Espoir, or as we call it, Hope. It's made up of other banished fae, who live in peace away from the mortals."

"Really?"

They rode through town. There were small cottages, each with a sign marking their trade. The farrier, the library, the butcher, and of course, the bakery.

"Their baker left last year, so they are very excited to meet their new one."

"Wait, what?" Rhea asked.

"I bought this for you. For us. You bake, I'll run the business side of things. What do you say?"

The unbridled joy on her face told him everything he needed to know. He stopped the horse, and she jumped down. She grabbed his hand and dragged him inside.

Rhea ran around, unable to withhold her excitement as she pointed out how she wanted things set up. Argus leaned against the doorway, arms crossed, and watched her, thinking of the children at winter solstice, eager to open their presents. She stopped and faced him.

"Is something funny?"

"You are, Princess." Her smile fell, and he crossed the room to her. "What's wrong?" he asked, taking her hand.

"Why did you call me that? You know I'm not a princess anymore."

"You will always be my princess."

"Really?"

"As long as we both shall live."

"Well, hello!"

They turned to see a fae entering. Rhea gasped. "Jessiah, is it really you?"

"Princess Wisteria," she offered with a bow. "Argus told us you were moving here. I had to see it for myself!"

"Why are you here?" Rhea asked.

"After you were discovered missing, your father blamed me. He banished me for not stopping you."

"Oh, I'm so sorry."

Jessiah smiled. "Don't be. I never would've met Thiery if you hadn't."

Rhea walked to her and hugged her. "I'm so glad there will be at least one fae here I know." Argus cleared his throat. Rhea laughed and rolled her eyes at him. "Besides you."

"Have you seen your cottage yet?" Jessiah asked.

"No, we just arrived."

"Go on and get settled in. I can be here in the morning to help get you started if you'd like."

"That would be great!"

Argus took Rhea's hand. "We'll see you then." They returned to the cart and traveled the path to their cottage.

Rhea shook her head at the sight of it. "This is too big for the two of us!" she exclaimed.

"Well, there is something we haven't really discussed yet."

"What are you talking about?"

"If we want to have a child or not."

"I never gave it much thought, since I was expected to provide an heir."

"Rhea, we don't have to do anything you don't want to."

"Let's enjoy our life together for now. We can discuss that later."

"Of course."

He helped her from her seat then lifted her up, carrying her across the threshold of their new home. They explored each room, with him taking her to their chamber last. She sighed at the sight of the bed.

"That looks so comfortable! I bet I'll sleep great on it."

"Hmm, I don't think you'll be getting much tonight," Argus said as he led her to the washroom. He opened the door, showing her the tub. "Shall we clean up and see what happens?"

"I like that idea."

He started the bath while she brought in a few bags. They sorted out what they would change into when they finished. He held her in the tub, tracing his fingers over her neck and chest.

Concern flooded him when she grew warm. "Rhea, what's wrong? Are you ill?"

She twisted so she straddled him, her face flush as she bit her lower lip. "You… We…"

"What?"

She giggled. "We haven't made love with me at full power."

Argus cocked his head. "I don't understand."

"You'll find out."

She stepped from the tub, drying herself then him when he joined her. In the bedroom, Argus attempted to light a fire. She pulled him back. With a snap of her fingers, the candles and fireplace roared to life. Argus could only chuckle.

He lifted her up, carried her to bed, and gently lay her on it before sliding up beside her. His lips pressed hers, before moving to her neck, her chest, and her stomach. She moaned softly as his tongue flicked her navel before moving lower.

"No, I need you. All of you, now," she begged.

"Whatever you need, my princess, I will always give you."

Her hips raised when he seated himself inside. He remained still for a moment, studying her.

"What?" she asked.

"Gods, did I ever tell you, you are the most beautiful creature to ever exist?" He wiped an unshed tear from her eye before they moved together, their body creating a symphony as heat flowed back and forth. He gripped her neck, his mouth devouring hers, when she trembled beneath him.

He joined her moments later, the rush of pleasure drawing out as she held him tightly. They lay in the aftermath, snuggling together as the evening light streamed in. She kissed him tenderly, breathing him in, and thanking the gods she finally had everything her heart longed for.

Epilogue

(One Year Later)

Rhea handed out the last loaf of bread, and once the customer left, Argus locked the door behind him.

"I think we can say today was a good day."

She smiled as she approached him. "Every day with you has been a good day."

"Oh, did you meet Sydrah? She is from the Water Court."

"I saw her but didn't get to meet her."

"Maybe tomorrow. Anyway, she told me a bit of news from the Faeryland Kingdom."

"Ooh, such as?"

He tried but failed to stifle his laugh. "The king decreed that after what happened at your ceremony with Mal, all binding ceremonies are now to be done in private. Only the couple and the priestess will be present."

Rhea couldn't help but laugh as well. "Gee, I wonder why."

"Also, with Mal's power gone, the peace has been maintained. At least for now."

"I'm glad to hear that."

"Now, Princess, about our discussion last night? Did you mean it, that you want to try?"

She thought for a moment before nodding in confirmation. "If it's what you want, I want it, too. There aren't many children here, but it's a wonderful place to raise a family. Regardless of what happens, I want you to know, this past year has been the happiest of my entire life. I am so happy with you, I don't think I could possibly put it all into words."

"That's all I need to know. As long as you are happy, loved, and fulfilled."

"You do all of that for me, and more."

They lived happily ever after...

The End

Acknowledgements:

To Kevin, I wouldn't be here without you.

To Jess, Steph, & Misty, thank you for being beta readers for this secret project. Your invaluable feedback means so much to me!

To my readers who were surprised to wake up and find out there was a new book. I hope you enjoyed it!

Thank you to everyone who helped support and promote this book on release day. I appreciate every single one of you.

About the Author

Autumn Kaufer bounces between the fae kingdoms and mortal realms when her schedule allows. When in the mortal realm, she can be found reading, writing, enjoying a walk through the woods, and spending time with her family.

If you've enjoyed this story, please check out The Stolen Royalty Series. Each story is a standalone fairytale retelling. Available anywhere books are sold.